HER DEADLY THREAT

BONZAI
MOON

BonzaiMoon Books LLC
Houston, Texas
www.bonzaimoonbooks.com

This is a work of fiction. Names, characters, places and incidents either are the product of the authors' imaginations or are used fictitiously, and any resemblance to actual persons, living or dead, business establishments, events, or locales is entirely coincidental.

Editing by Kelly Hartigan of Xterra Web
http://editing.xterraweb.com

1

Staring at her reflection in the framed mirror above the dresser, Spencer took several deep breaths and tried to calm down. Since her conversation with Ben yesterday afternoon, she'd been consumed with how she would accomplish *Step Three*. So far, the GHB seemed to be her best option.

Spencer didn't want to use the GHB.

But she had to.

Because of that damn blue file with the photos John had taken of her.

John's suspicions might hinder her search for the envelope Ben wanted. The only way to remove those hindrances would be to drug John. Spencer glanced at the vial of GHB and then at her reflection, hating herself for what she was going to do, but she didn't have a choice. If she didn't find that damn envelope, then—

I can't guarantee that I won't burn your grandmother's house to the ground, and I can't guarantee that she won't be at home when I strike the match.

She had to use the GHB, or Ben would hurt her grandmother. Taking a deep breath, Spencer tried to calm down, but it wasn't working. Nothing would stop her heart from slamming. Not when she couldn't stop thinking about *Step Three.*

I want you to pour him a glass of wine, and then pour the contents of the vial I sent you into the wine. Once he has passed out, find the envelope, and then call me. I'll tell you what to do next when I hear from you. I know you can do it, so don't disappoint me. I'm not asking you to do anything that you haven't done before.

Ben was right. She had drugged men before. Today, she would have to do it again. Spencer knew she could, but it wouldn't be easy. It never was.

Unlike Rae, Spencer had never mastered the art of remaining calm while watching a man drain a glass of drugged wine. She usually had to force herself to go through with it, but it was always damn near impossible to convince herself that she could actually unscrew the top off the vial and pour the liquid into the glass of wine.

Most times, she'd have to trick herself into drugging the guy and pretend she was acting in some movie. Still, she was always tense and nauseous, waiting for the man to succumb to the effects of the drug and slump over, unconscious.

She stared at the vial of GHB.

I'm not asking you to do anything that you haven't done before …

Spencer took another long, deep breath. No more hesitating, it was time to—

No, she couldn't do it, not this time.

She couldn't drug John. Cursing, Spencer grabbed the vial, glaring at it. The GHB seemed to stare back at her, mocking her, warning her, congratulating her.

You can't do it, you dumb bitch. You've gotten too close; you've fallen in love with him and for what? So he can break your heart when he finds out you're a lying, thieving bitch?

You have to do it, or you'll never find the envelope, and Ben will kill your grandmother, the woman who loved you when your own mother abandoned you! Her death will be your fault!

You can't drug John. It isn't right. You can't keep making bad decisions and stupid mistakes. You do have a choice. You don't have to steal or lie!

The thoughts played over and over in her mind.

Finally, no longer able to stand the horrible, dizzying mantra, Spencer hurled the vial against the wall.

2

San Ignacio, Belize

Belizean Banyan Resort - Owner's Casita

Sione opened the door and found himself a bit speechless.

Ms. Edwards stood on the porch outside his casita, at a little past two in the afternoon, wearing the pink sarong she'd bought on their trip to San Pedro. He remembered her having problems figuring out how to tie it, but she seemed to have done a fairly decent job by herself and had somehow managed to showcase her cleavage. She looked beautiful, just like he remembered. Not that he'd forgotten or could ever forget.

"Hi." She smiled a little.

"Hi." He smiled back, just a little, no more than she did. He didn't want her to think he was happy to see her, or anything, even though he might have been glad she was at his door. He was a bit upset about her disappearing act yesterday morning. Ms. Edwards had left the kitchen when D.J. arrived, claiming she was going off to take a shower.

After what D.J. had told him about the Xanax box he'd found in Maxine Porter's closet, Sione had toyed with the idea of questioning Ms. Edwards about the fake passports and money she'd delivered to Carla Garcia, Karen Nelson, and Maxine Porter. By the time his cousin had left, Ms. Edwards was gone.

"Don't mean to bother you," Spencer said. "But I think I left my earrings in the guest room when I stayed here last night."

Sione nodded, thinking it might be a good time to find out what Ms. Edwards had to say about the money and fake passports. He wasn't sure he wanted to interrogate her right this moment. He wasn't sure how to pose the questions he needed answers to.

"My grandmother gave me those earrings. They're really special to me." Ms. Edwards looked a bit irritated as a jungle breeze blew a strand of hair across her face. "Would it be okay if I looked for them?"

Sione stepped back, allowing her to enter. "Sure, no problem."

As she walked into the foyer, he tried to remind himself that she wasn't the kind of woman he wanted to get involved with, no matter how beautiful she was. If Ms. Edwards was mixed up with fake passports and illicit money, it would be best to stay away from her. The problem was, Sione didn't want to stay away. He actually wanted to get a bit closer.

3

San Ignacio, Belize
Belizean Banyan Resort - Owner's Casita

Spencer slipped into John's master bedroom and then closed the doors behind her.

Taking a deep breath, she stood still, waiting for her blood pressure to lower, praying she wouldn't have a stroke. It was probably crazy to be in his bedroom, without his permission, when he could walk in at any time. But she had to look for the envelope. She had to find the envelope.

Showing up on his doorstep today had been a gamble. Spencer half-expected he would deny her access, but he'd allowed her entry, and she had to make the most of it, especially since he was still in the casita, alert and conscious, not slumped over somewhere, suffering the effects of GHB.

She'd been determined not to drug John, despite Ben's orders, even though it might have made things easier for her.

The lie she'd told John about missing earrings had taken a toll—emotionally and physically. She was literally on the verge of a nervous breakdown, but she couldn't fall apart.

In addition to John's bedroom, Spencer had only two more to search. Hopefully, she would find the envelope. *Step Three* would be done, she could give the envelope to Ben, he would give her the video, and she could leave Belize and never look back.

And never see John again.

Spencer moved from the door and dashed to the large walk-in closet, a long, thin rectangle with racks of clothes on either side. At the back was a huge armoire against the wall, a massive piece of furniture with two doors and three drawers at the bottom. Spencer hurried to the armoire and eased to her knees on the cool hardwood floor in front of it, staring at the drawers.

She couldn't help but remember the night she'd opened that drawer in Ben Chang's closet, unaware of the hell she was unleashing in her life. Why hadn't she known what Ben was capable of then? Why hadn't she seen the signs? Looking back, with twenty-twenty hindsight of course, she realized all the evidence had been there. The guns. The money. Why hadn't she made the conclusions? Maybe the better question was why hadn't she wanted to make those conclusions?

Spencer opened the bottom drawer and pushed aside the assortment of T-shirts. Pulling the drawer out farther, she pushed aside more T-shirts. Near the back corner of the drawer was a square of chamois. Peeking beneath the edge of it was a strange sickle-shaped object, hard and black, with a razor-sharp point.

Spencer lifted the soft cloth. Gasping, she stared at four long claws, which seemed to be welded, or fused somehow, on top of what looked like a set of brass knuckles. Her heart slamming, she picked up the claws. What the hell? Why did John have these strange claws in his drawer? What were they used for?

The severed hand, covered with blood, in Maxine Porter's closet invaded her mind. Horrified by the potential direction of her thoughts, Spencer put the claws back were she'd found them and slammed the drawer.

Shuddering, Spencer pulled out the second drawer, trying to push the image of those strange claws from her mind. Struggling to forget the questions swirling in her head, she focused on the contents in the second drawer.

A compass, a bundle of letters, an old cigar box, a Mont Blanc pen, and a faded three-by-five picture of a woman, an exotic island girl with sun-kissed caramel skin and long, thick, black hair swept over one shoulder. She turned the photo over and saw a name scribbled on the back. *Moana.* Spencer flipped the photo and stared at the exotic beauty. Was this the old girlfriend? The woman who wouldn't stop calling? The woman he claimed he didn't want to talk to? The woman he'd broken his promise to? Or, maybe—

"Ms. Edwards."

Startled, Spencer looked back over her shoulder, heart pounding.

John stood in the entrance to the closet, frowning at her. "What are you doing in here?"

Panicked, she shoved the photo back into the drawer and then closed it. "Nothing," she stammered, her voice barely above a whisper. "I was just ..."

"Just?"

Letting out a slow, silent exhale, Spencer stood and turned to him. With two long strides, John was inches from her, staring at her, making her uncomfortable with his piercing gaze, as if he was trying to figure her out, or size her up. Spencer forced herself to stare back, to match his gaze, trying to summon up a sly sassiness. The truth was, she was shaking in her boots.

"I thought you said your earrings were in the guest bedroom?" John asked, his gaze and his tone holding traces of suspicion.

"I checked the guest bedroom, but they weren't there," she said. "Then I remembered that I left the guest room and spent the night in your room ... with you ... so I decided to check in your closet because I got the T-shirt from your closet, remember?"

"I remember," he said, his gaze still piercing.

"Because I needed something to sleep in ..." she said, trying not to stammer, wondering if he believed her story.

"Did you find your earrings?"

"No, I didn't," she said and then ventured to walk around him, desperate to get the hell out of the closet.

John stepped in front of her. Swallowing, Spencer stepped back, looking up at him.

"What do the earrings look like?"

Spencer took a quick breath. "Oh, um ... they're just little pearls. Not expensive or anything."

Nodding, he said, "I'll tell the housekeeping staff to look out for them."

4

As Sione escorted her out of his bedroom, two thoughts dominated his mind. One, Ms. Edwards had lied to him. Her story about missing pearl earrings was bullshit. Although, he had to admit, it was a pretty good cover. Special earrings given to her by the grandmother who'd raised her after her mother died. Of course, she'd want to look for them.

But Ms. Edwards hadn't returned to his casita to look for misplaced jewelry. She had come back to look for something though. Damn if he knew what. Sione sighed as his second thought eclipsed his first. Ms. Edwards looked just as good from behind as she did from the front. He told himself that didn't matter. He couldn't get caught up in her beauty, because—

Excited shrieks made his heart jump for a second. Turning toward the commotion, he saw his little second cousins, Keisha, Maggie, and India, racing down the hall toward them.

"Miss Spencer! Miss Spencer!" the girls squealed and giggled, dashing over to Ms. Edwards, all three of them trying to throw their arms around her.

Setting her purse on the accent table in the foyer, Ms. Edwards eased to her knees, eye level to them, and hugged them back. She matched the girls' squeals and giggles and seemed to enjoy all the attention they lavished on her. Sione found it hard to reconcile the woman who was so affectionate with his second cousins and the woman who might have been mixed up in something illegal.

Finally, Ms. Edwards stood. Two of the girls grabbed her hands, while the third latched on to her elbow, and they began to drag her out of the foyer, excitedly announcing all the plans they had to spend the afternoon playing and inviting her to join them.

"Wait, wait," Ms. Edwards told the girls. "We need to ask your cousin if it's okay for me to play with you."

Immediately, the girls turned to Sione and began shouting their wishes. "We want Miss Spencer to play with us!" the girls pleaded, though there was an undercurrent of command in their high-pitched pleas. "Let her stay and play with us!"

Sighing, Sione crossed his arms, looking down at the cute little expectant faces staring up at him, waiting for his answer. Of course, he knew he couldn't say "no," or there would be hell to pay, bitter tears and threats of retaliation.

He wasn't sure he liked the idea of Ms. Edwards playing with his second cousins.

The recent revelations about her were damaging and, if he were honest with himself, more than a bit disappointing. Sione could no longer give Ms. Edwards the benefit of the doubt because there was no proof that money and passports had been in the bags she'd switched.

D.J. had found the Xanax box in Maxine Porter's closet, which meant Ms. Edwards had made the delivery to the store clerk. Sione couldn't pretend Ms. Edwards was innocent anymore. Yet he didn't like the view of Ms. Edwards as deceptive and manipulative. He was having trouble wrapping his mind around the idea of her as a criminal.

The longing look in Spencer Edwards' eyes as she smiled at the girls made him think of her childhood. The brief glances she'd allowed him so far were of a lonely, neglected little girl. Knowing firsthand the effects of a troubled upbringing, Sione was inclined to think he might be wrong about her. Maybe the situation with the fake money and passports wasn't so black and white. Maybe there was a reason for her involvement, one that could be explained, understood, and even accepted.

Glancing at Ms. Edwards, Sione had a feeling she wanted to stay and play with the girls just as much as they wanted her to. If he didn't allow the "play date," she might be more upset than the girls. On a practical note, he hadn't planned to babysit today. His cousin Terrance, the girls' father, had caught him off guard with the request, and Sione hadn't said no, even though he was behind on a lot of paperwork.

He had invoices to approve, more résumés for the pool assistant position to review, and business proposals to consider. It would help him out if Ms. Edwards could keep the girls occupied while he got some work done.

"Can Miss Spencer stay and play with us?" Maggie ran to him, giving him the sweetest, toothless smile. "Please?"

Unable to resist, Sione reached down, picked Maggie up, and

kissed her cheek. "Yes, love, Miss Spencer can stay and play with you and your sisters."

Happy and excited, Keisha and India cheered and clapped, and when Sione looked over at Ms. Edwards, the smile she gave him was even sweeter.

5

Sione stood just outside the arched entryway into the kitchen. Ms. Edwards and the girls sat at the large round table in the breakfast nook, giggling and talking, the four of them creating some type of art project. The table was littered with large sheets of construction paper in every color, pencils, markers, stickers, glue, watercolors, scissors, and glitter.

It was an inviting, happy scene, and Sione felt a strange stirring, a longing for a family of his own and a situation where he would walk into the kitchen and his wife and kids would be sitting at the table. It was odd, and a bit disturbing, that Ms. Edwards could make him feel that way. A woman mixed up in something shady and criminal should have inspired suspicion and mistrust, not blissful domesticity.

"What's all this?" Sione walked into the kitchen. "What are you girls making? A big mess that I'm going to have to clean up?"

"It's not a mess," India said, her chin smudged with green paint.

Smiling, Maggie announced, "We're making a masterpiece!"

"A masterpiece, huh?" Sione went to the table, giving each of the girls a playful thump on the forehead, which they laughingly protested, and he checked out the drawings the girls were making—houses, stick people, flowers, balloons, and a few shapes he couldn't quite figure out.

"And what about you, Ms. Edwards?" Sione glanced over at the piece of paper Ms. Edwards was sketching on, a scene which seemed to include palm trees and blue skies. "You making a masterpiece or a mess?"

Making a face at him, Spencer Edwards stuck out her tongue, then smiled, and said, "Maggie, what is that you're drawing? A birthday cake?"

"A wedding cake!" Maggie said.

"A wedding cake?" Ms. Edwards exclaimed. "Are you getting married and you didn't tell me? Let me see your hand! Do you have an engagement ring?"

"No!" Maggie giggled. "I can't get married."

"You have to have a boyfriend to get married," Keisha said, rolling her eyes at her sister.

"Miss Spencer, do you have a husband?" India asked.

"Do you have a boyfriend?" Maggie asked, giggling.

"Um, no," Ms. Edwards said. "I don't."

"But you're so pretty," India said. "You should have someone to be in love with!"

"And you can love him," Keisha teased and then laughed.

"And you can kiss him," Maggie said, smacking her lips, imitating kissing sounds.

"Girls," Sione warned.

The girls kept giggling, and then India said, "Miss Spencer, you can marry cousin Sione. He doesn't have a wife. He's all alone and Auntie Carmen says that's a crying shame because she doesn't have any grandbabies."

"Girls!" Sione said, his tone gruff though he realized they were only repeating opinions they'd heard from his mother.

Maggie scowled at him. "Don't you want a wife?"

"Miss Spencer could be a pretty wife for you," Keisha said.

"Maggie, are you drawing a butterfly?" Ms. Edwards asked, effectively changing the subject, for which Sione was grateful.

Their focus redirected, the girls continued their drawings, and Ms. Edwards kept them engaged in animated conversations on topics more appropriate for six-to-seven-year-old little girls.

Maggie announced, "I'm going to give my masterpiece to Mommy."

"I'm going to give mine to Mommy, too." India promised, grabbing a green crayon.

"Me, too!" said Keisha, not to be outdone.

"Miss Spencer," Maggie said. "Are you going to give your picture to your mommy, too?"

"What?" Ms. Edwards' pencil skidded across the paper, creating a haphazard line, ruining the sailboat she'd been drawing.

"Miss Spencer!" Keisha said. "You messed up your picture!"

Dropping the pencil, Ms. Edwards looked at the girls, obviously struggling to speak. "I just, um, I ..."

Confused by her disorientation, Sione became concerned as tears welled in Ms. Edwards' eyes. The girls noticed her distress too and immediately began asking her what was the matter, their faces filled with tension and worry.

Instead of answering the girls, Ms. Edwards pushed the chair back from the table, stood, and ran out of the kitchen.

Near tears themselves, the girls jumped up to follow her, but Sione stopped them. "Stay here, I'll go and see if she's okay."

Sione left the kitchen, worried that the girls' conversation about their mother had reminded Ms. Edwards of her mother's death and had triggered the tears. Heading down the hall, he rounded the corner into the foyer and saw Ms. Edwards walking toward the door.

"Ms. Edwards …"

She glanced over her shoulder at him, then turned back to the door, and grabbed the knob.

"Wait a minute." Sione grabbed her arm and forced her to face him. "What's wrong? Are you crying because—"

"I'm not crying." She yanked away from him and then swiped at the tears with trembling fingers. "It's just allergies."

Gently, he lifted her chin. Forcing her to look at him, he wiped away a tear she missed. "I don't believe you."

"Please tell the girls I had fun with them, but …" She took a deep breath and looked up at him. "I'm just not feeling well, and I don't want them to think I abandoned them or I'm disappointed with them about something."

"Listen, I know it was probably difficult for you to hear the girls talking about their mother when—"

"I have to go." She opened the door and hurried out.

6

"John?" Ms. Edwards stared at him, confusion in her brown eyes. "What are you doing here?"

Sione stared at her, amazed at how innocent and vulnerable she seemed in a pair of pajamas and slippers. She looked much younger without the makeup and her hair swirling around her shoulders, loose and wavy, free from the severe hairstyle she usually wore.

"I was just ..." Sione wondered if he'd made a mistake, showing up at her casita unannounced. "I was worried about you."

"You were?" She gave him a skeptical look.

"I mean, the girls were worried," he amended. "Because of what happened this afternoon."

"They shouldn't be worried about me," she said. "I told you to tell them I wasn't feeling well."

"They didn't believe that," he said. "And I didn't either."

Smiling a little, she leaned against the door and stared up at him. "I'll be fine. So don't worry, okay?"

"Well, since you're okay," Sione sighed. "I should probably leave. I'm sorry I bothered you."

"Do I look bothered?"

Was that a trick question? Wary, he said, "I don't know …"

"Come on in." Ms. Edwards sighed, then turned, and headed into the living area, allowing him to follow her. Against his better judgment, Sione crossed the threshold and closed the door behind him.

"Want some wine? Compliments of the resort." Ms. Edwards walked into the kitchen and headed to the refrigerator. "Which means you paid for it, so …"

"Sure." Sione went to the couch and sat.

She opened the pinot noir and poured them each a few ounces into wine glasses.

"Here you go." She handed him a glass, joining him on the couch. Ms. Edwards tapped her glass against his, took a healthy gulp and then asked, "Were you really worried about me?"

"Yes." Sione put his glass on the coffee table.

"Why?" Staring at him, she held the rim of the glass against her mouth and then took a small sip of wine. "You don't even know me."

"Well, maybe I want to get to know you."

It was probably a good time to talk about the contents of those Xanax boxes, to find out if she would come clean or if she would lie to him. But Sione wasn't in the mood to take her through some sort of "Belizean Inquisition". He still had every intention of asking her about the fake passports and money, but maybe not tonight. Right now, he just wanted to enjoy some wine with a beautiful woman he wanted to know more about.

She took another sip of wine and put the glass on the coffee table. "What do you want to know about me?"

Smiling a bit, he asked, "Have you ever been in love, Ms. Edwards?"

She glanced at him, and he saw the slight panic in her eyes before she reached for the wine glass again. "Why would you ask me that?"

"You told me that you weren't going to fall in love and waste your time on someone just to have it blow up in your face," he reminded her. "So, I thought, maybe you had been in love before, but it ended badly."

"No, that's not it," she cut him off, her tone curt. "I mean, I don't think I really know what love is, so I doubt I've ever been in it."

"Then why are you so sure that you don't want to fall in love?" He angled toward her, eager to move closer. "Have you ever thought that if you ever did fall in love, you might like it?"

Frowning, she finished off the pinot noir, then put the empty glass on the coffee table, and looked at him, a slight challenge in her stare. "Have you ever been in love, John?"

"No," he admitted, meeting her gaze. "But I am looking forward to it."

She stared at him, with the same doe-in-the-headlights look she'd given him out by the pool. It was almost as if she was dealing with some internal struggle, waging a war against herself that she would never win, and yet she had to fight.

Sione could relate to her discomfort. He was regularly beset by his own internal struggles, moments where he fought to make sure the secrets he kept hidden didn't spill out all over the place.

She grabbed the empty glass and then stood. "I'll tell you what I'm looking forward to."

"What's that?"

She smiled. "More wine."

7

____

San Ignacio, Belize
Belizean Banyan Resort - Honeymoon Casita

"You believe in love at first sight Ms. Edwards?" John asked.

Leaning against the throw pillow from the couch, Spencer stared up at the ceiling, her eyes following the crown molding along the perimeter of the room. She and John had already finished one bottle of wine and were sprawled out on the floor in the living area of her casita, working on the second bottle.

Perplexed, Spencer looked at John, lying inches away from her, hands behind his head. "Are you serious?"

"Do you?"

"Not exactly." Spencer grabbed the nearly empty bottle of pinot noir on the floor between them.

"Why not?"

Spencer took a healthy swig from the bottle and said, "Love at first sight never happens."

"Never?" He glanced at her.

"Never." She put the bottle down. "Love at first sight is just wishful thinking."

"So, you don't think," John started, his tone hypothetical, "that you could see someone and fall instantly in love?"

Spencer laughed. "Fall instantly in love? John, you are so way beyond drunk! No more wine for you."

"You had more than I did," he insisted, sitting up and grabbing the bottle. "And there's hardly any left in here. You drank all of this one."

"I did not," Spencer protested. "I drank all of the last bottle, but we shared that bottle in your hand."

Sighing, John put the bottle down. "So, you don't think you could see someone, and just know, someway, somehow, that you belong with that person, you want to be with that person, and no matter what it takes, you'll find a way to be with them."

"Love at first sight is a silly myth," she said. "Besides, I already told you, I don't plan to get caught up in love."

"What's wrong with getting caught up in love?" Sione asked, resting his head on a corner of Spencer's pillow.

Moving her head to give him a bit more room, she sighed and then said, "Nothing, except …"

"Except?"

"What about you?" she said, desperate to change the subject. "Are you ready to get caught up in love?"

John moved so that he was lying on his back and just a bit too close to her than she wanted him to be.

"I am," he said. "I want to fall in love with someone and spend the rest of my life with her."

She turned her head toward him. "The rest of your life is a really long time."

John laughed.

"So, what kind of woman would Mrs. Tuiali'i be?"

"Hopefully, she'll be a compassionate, loving woman who cares about other people, selfless and sincere," he said. "She'll be smart and have her own opinions, but she won't be judgmental. She'll be honest, someone I can trust, someone who will help me be a better person."

Spencer sighed softly, thinking about what he wanted in a woman. He'd described the exact opposite of her, and it bothered her, knowing the kind of woman she would have to be if she wanted to be with John. She could never be that woman. She would never live up to his expectations. The realization angered her and made her long for something she had convinced herself she didn't want.

"You think that's too much to ask?"

Spencer turned to face him, not entirely surprised to find him facing her. There were only scant inches between them. "You won't have a problem finding a Mrs. Tuiali'i."

"Really?"

"I know you won't," she said, aware of the inches between them disappearing as she moved closer to him. "Because you're very charitable and accommodating."

"Charitable and accommodating." He frowned. "You think I'm nice?"

"I think you're beautiful," Spencer said, her words a bit slurred, and the amusement in his gaze worried her because "beautiful" was probably the wrong word choice, but she would blame it on the wine.

"Really?"

"Mm-hmm," she said and slipped an arm around his waist, moving closer, getting rid of what remaining space was left between them.

"You have beautiful eyes," she said, planting a whisper-soft kiss against his eyelid, something she couldn't do if she weren't totally drunk. And beautiful skin," she said, trailing kisses along his jaw. "And a beautiful mouth." Without thinking of the ramifications, she leaned forward until her mouth was inches from his.

"Ms. Edwards," John whispered against her lips.

"Spencer," she whispered back.

"What?"

"You can call me Spencer." Gently, she placed her hands on either side of his face, and kissed him again. With a lot less reluctance. And a lot more tumult.

A bit frantic, she moved on top of him and kissed him as though her life depended on it, as if she were thirsting for him. *I have to stop this.* She knew that. But his mouth was so delicious, sweet and ripe.

John stopped the kiss and asked, "Are you sure you should be doing this?"

Breathless, she shook her head, gazing at his full lips. "No."

"Then why are you kissing me?"

"Maybe I'm drunk." Spencer kissed him again.

An intense urgency to have him inside her took over, consumed her, and she slid her hand along the front of his pants, slipping her fingers beneath the waistband. Without warning, John grabbed her wrist, yanked her hand away, grabbed her other hand, and pinned her to the floor on her back.

"What's the matter?" she asked, her heart racing in anticipation.

"I don't think this is a good idea," he said, much too serious.

"Why not?" She glanced down below his waist again.

"Because ..." He frowned a bit.

"Never mind." Humiliated, disappointed, Spencer looked away. "It doesn't matter."

John released her and then stood, grabbing the empty wine bottle. "I'm going to put this away."

Confused and mortified, Spencer jumped up and wobbled over toward the table in the kitchen nook. God, what the hell was her problem? Why did she ask him "why not?" It was obvious why not. He didn't know her and he didn't trust her. He was suspicious of her. He'd followed her to the Mayan ruins and took photos of her that he was probably going to give to the police.

"Spencer."

Her stomach flipped and then flopped.

John's presence behind her embraced her even before his arms encircled her. "I don't want you to think that I don't want to be with you because I do …"

She leaned back against his chest, enveloped in his warmth.

"It's just …" Sione tried to continue.

Turning in his embrace, Spencer stood on her toes, winding her arms around his neck. "It's just what?"

Sighing, he said, "I didn't come here to try to get you into bed."

"I wouldn't mind if you had."

His gaze a bit regretful, John removed her arms. Worried he might see disappointment in her gaze, Spencer half-walked, half-staggered over to the refrigerator, opened it, and grabbed the last bottle of wine.

"Three's the charm," she said, upset because she was disappointed.

"Maybe we've had enough for tonight," John suggested.

Spencer sighed, thinking about the way his mouth felt against hers, wondering if fermented grapes would make the intense longing go away. "John, I haven't had nearly enough."

8

San Ignacio, Belize

Belizean Banyan Resort - Honeymoon Casita

Spencer's eyes opened, slowly. With confusion and shock, she realized her left cheek was resting against John's chest, which was hard and warm, his heartbeat strong and steady. Spencer felt his thumb glide gently along her thumb, and when she tilted her head down, she stared at their intertwined fingers.

"You awake?" John asked.

"Um … I think," Spencer said, pulling her hand from his and wiping her mouth. "How long have I been asleep?"

"About nine hours," he said.

Frantic, she stared at him, hoping he wasn't serious. "Nine *hours?*"

"It's ten thirty-seven … in the morning."

"Oh my God, I can't believe you let me sleep that long." Raising up from the pillow, she stared at him. "Wait a minute. Why are you in my bed?"

"That last bottle of wine knocked you out," he said. "And I was a bit drunk, too, so—"

"A bit?" she challenged, raking fingers through her tangled hair.

Sheepishly, he laughed softly. "Okay, I was very drunk. We both were and I couldn't remember how to get back to my casita. Then you said I shouldn't venture out into the jungle and risk being attacked by a jaguar, and I'm glad."

"Because you might have been attacked by a jaguar?"

"Because I might not have been here when you woke up this morning," he said, gazing at her. "Next to me."

Her gaze dropped to his chest and she stared at the ink etched into his brown sugary skin. "And yet, you were sober enough to take your shirt off?" Spencer asked, examining his chest, trying to make sense of the tattoos.

John shrugged. "I didn't think you'd mind."

She looked at him. "Excuse me?"

Smiling, he said, "You've already seen me with my shirt off."

Spencer sighed. "What do all those tattoos mean anyway?"

"It's a story," he said.

"A story?"

"Come here." John reached for her.

Wary, Spencer leaned away from his grasp. "Why?"

"I'm going to tell you the story." He took her hand, pulling her into his personal space, so close she could feel the warmth from his skin.

Honestly, she was too close, but she couldn't seem to figure out how to move away.

"See the tattoo on my neck," he said. "The story starts there. Long, long ago—"

"How long ago is long, long ago?" Spencer asked, gazing at the parabolic-shaped whorls swirling down his neck and over his shoulders.

"I'd say a pretty long time ago," he said, quite serious, though she had a feeling he was trying not to smile. "Way, way before you were born, definitely."

"That long, huh?"

John laughed a bit, boyish and adorable, and Spencer felt her stomach gearing up for the onslaught of a thousand butterflies.

"Okay, so, a long time before you were born," he started again, "a good and noble man, who cared very much for his people, was betrayed, tricked into giving up the most precious thing to him."

"Which was what?" She glanced at her fingernails.

"His love," John said, in a tone so solemn, she couldn't help but look up at him.

She felt like a fool as he grinned, snickering at her. Crossing her arms, she said, "Go on."

"So he left his village," Sione said. "Set out on a pilgrimage, seeking love, so he could help his people because without love, he was no good to them."

"How unfortunate," she said, trying not to hang on to every word.

"He searched and searched—"

"And searched?" Spencer supplied, giggling.

"And searched," he confirmed and then grabbed her hand. "And finally, after a long, long time of searching—"

"And searching some more," she said, trying to keep things light, trying to ignore the effects of his voice and his fingers mingling with hers.

"He came across a beautiful girl," he said, "and when he saw her, he knew he had found love and he would be restored, but she was afraid of him."

"Why?" Spencer asked, following the swirling patterns along his arms and chest, looking for the good and noble man and the beautiful girl.

"She was afraid of the love inside of her," he said, looking at her. "And even though she knew the love was there, she spent most of her time trying to hide it, pretending it wasn't there, because she was afraid to share that love."

"Maybe she had a reason for that," she countered, feeling a bit defensive for some reason. "Love is dangerous."

He gave her an odd look. "Dangerous?"

"There is an element of danger in love," she said, thinking of her mother. "It's dangerous to love someone. It's dangerous to be loved. I mean, that's my opinion, anyway. Finish your story."

"Well, the beautiful girl was afraid to love him," he said. "So, she ran away."

"And he ran after her?"

"No," he said. "He let her go."

"I don't understand." She shook her head. "Why didn't he go after her? Why didn't he just take what he wanted?"

"He wanted to wait until she was ready to love him," he explained, serious again, without the silly smile. "He couldn't make her love him because love is patient and kind, you know, so he waited."

"And she came back?"

"He's still waiting." He drew her attention to an odd pattern that stopped just above his navel.

"He's still waiting?"

Chuckling, John said, "The tattoo isn't finished."

"So, there's no end to this story?"

John shrugged. "Well, I'm guessing she'll eventually come back and decide to love him, but who knows."

Spencer sighed. "Um ... listen ... I think we need to talk about something."

"Something?"

"About what happened between us last night."

"What are you talking about?"

"The kiss," she said. "It shouldn't have happened."

"Why not?" he asked, grinning. "Didn't you like it?"

"Maybe I liked it a *little* bit," Spencer admitted, scooting away from him. "Still, it doesn't matter. It can never happen again."

Sione grabbed her wrist, stopping her. "Why can't it?"

Spencer stared at him, knowing it was a waste of time to fantasize about being with him, knowing they could never be together. She wasn't on vacation, engaging in some kind of wanton jungle fling. She was being forced to do a "favor" for Ben Chang. And she would have to deal with the threat of the cops banging on her door to question her about the money and watches she'd stolen if she didn't do what Ben told her to do.

Find the envelope.

"Because you don't believe in love and romance and all that foolishness, right?" Sione ran a hand down the back of his head.

"I can't get involved with anyone right now," Spencer said.

"Are we getting involved?" he asked, his smile sly.

Frustrated, she shook her head. "Now is not a good time for me to fall in love."

"So, you're planning on falling in love with me?"

"I can't start anything with you, John, because I won't be able to finish it."

"What does that mean?"

Spencer swung her legs over the side of the bed and then stood. "It means—"

Three loud chimes cut through the cozy, lazy morning

atmosphere. Spencer froze for a few seconds, knowing the significance of the chirping.

Sione sat up. "What was that?"

"Um … it's my phone." Heart pounding, Spencer hurried to the dresser across from the bed and opened the Birkin sitting on the mahogany surface. Reaching into the purse, she grabbed the burner phone and retrieved the text.

Have you found the envelope, sweet girl

Her heart punching, Spencer glanced back at John and found him staring at her.

"Um, it's a text from my sister," she said. "Give me a sec."

A wave of apprehension washed over Spencer as she re-read the text once and then again, her legs threatening to give way beneath her. Ben wanted to know if Step Three was complete. What the hell was she supposed to tell him? She hadn't really thought about the damn envelope. She was too busy being hung over and distracted by some silly love story told in the tattoos spread across John's muscular chest. Her face flaming with panic and guilt, she sent a reply, fingers moving furiously over the miniature keyboard.

Still looking

The burner phone trembled in her hand. Waiting for the reply, Spencer glanced back at John, trying to read the look he was giving her as he grabbed his shirt from a side chair near the French doors before making his way back toward her.

The burner phone chimed again. Spencer read the message: *sweet girl, you need to use the GHB. Drug him and find that damn envelope!*

"Everything okay?" John asked, maneuvering his head through the opening in the tan polo shirt and then slipping his arms into the short sleeves.

"Yeah." She gazed up at him, fighting the urge to lean against him and let him envelop her in his warm, protective embrace. "Just my sister complaining about her boyfriend."

"Listen." He slipped an arm around her, pulling her closer to him. "I know you don't need a hero and you don't want anyone to fight your battles, but ..."

"But?"

"I really think it would be best if you came back to my casita," he said.

"Why?" she asked, trying to read his hazel eyes, suspicious of his motives. "You really think that Asian guy is going to come back and try to hurt me again?"

She wanted to ask, *Do you want me to come back to your casita because it would be easier to watch me? Are you just trying to find out why I had money and fake passports delivered to me?*

"I don't think we should tempt fate," he said. "Besides, I wasn't able to get the surveillance guys out last week, so they're coming tomorrow to install more cameras around the area."

Nodding, Spencer said, "Maybe it does make sense for me to stay with you."

She wasn't really sure. Maybe John just wanted to keep tabs on her and was looking for proof to confirm his doubts about her. She wasn't going to put up a fight, though. She needed unrestricted access to his casita to look for that envelope.

"Why don't you pack your things," he said. "I'll send someone to pick you up in about an hour."

9

San Ignacio, Belize

Belizean Banyan Resort - Honeymoon Casita

Moments after John left the honeymoon casita, Spencer returned to the bed and stretched across the duvet, heading for the pillow John had fallen asleep on. Despite feeling foolish, she grabbed the pillow. It smelled like him, and for a few seconds, she pressed her face against the downy softness and imagined he was still with her. For a moment, she felt as though she were waking up in his arms again, residing in his embrace, listening to that silly story of the tattoo, which she figured he'd made up.

That tale of love was most likely his indictment of her opinions on love and romance. He probably thought she was afraid to fall in love, and maybe he was right, but she didn't think she deserved to have stones thrown at her because she was scared of losing her identity and her dignity and everything else that was important and fundamental.

Spencer had seen her mother go down that lonely road. She didn't want to follow, and she wasn't about to take one step down the path of heartbreak and self-deprecation.

Spencer tossed the pillow away, sat up, and scrambled off the bed. Tonight, she was moving into John's casita, but she was conflicted. On the one hand, she was wary and nervous. John knew she'd lied about the contents of the banker's box. She was sure of it. She was just as sure that he'd opened the Xanax boxes and had found the money and passports. And somehow, someway, he'd found out about the side venture. He'd known she was going to Xunantunich to switch bags with a woman named Carla Garcia, so he'd followed her and took photos of her every move.

She couldn't help but wonder if the invitation to stay with him was some kind of setup, but part of her was giddy and excited. Thinking about being with him, remembering how it felt to fall asleep in his arms and to wake up in his arms, made her wish she were moving in with him under different circumstances. Pushing away the silly fantasies, Spencer grabbed the burner phone and frowned when she saw the onslaught of texts from Ben. She decided to call him.

"I do not like being ignored, sweet girl," he said as soon as he answered. "Don't play games with me. When I call you, or text you, I expect—"

"I haven't found the envelope, but don't worry." She walked back to the bed. "I'm moving in with Sione Tuiali'i."

"Moving in with him?"

"I'm going to be staying in the owner's casita while more cameras are put up around the honeymoon casita," she said. "It was his idea."

There was silence, followed by a clipped exhale, and then he said, "Sweet girl, I must say, I'm impressed."

Wary of the strange tension in his tone, she said, "Well, you wanted me to get unrestricted access to his casita, right?"

"Is that what you are giving him? Unrestricted access?" Ben asked. "Is that why he asked you to move in with him?"

Sitting on the edge of the bed, Spencer said, "You wanted me to get close to him."

"But not too close," he reminded her.

"What do you care how close I get to him?" Spencer asked. "As long as I find that damn envelope."

"Believe it or not, and you probably won't," Ben said. "But I don't want you to be disappointed, sweet girl."

"What are you talking about?"

"Sione may appreciate your beauty, sweet girl," Ben said. "But he will never choose to be with a woman like you."

"A woman like me?"

"Sione was influenced by a good man, a very pious man," Ben said. "And that man warned him that a disgraceful woman is like cancer in a man's bones. Sione will heed that warning."

"Who the hell says I want him to choose me?" she asked. "Who says I'm interested in him?"

"Sweet girl, don't make the mistake of getting too close to Sione Tuiali'i," Ben said. "He won't want you when he learns that you are a liar and a thief."

10

San Ignacio, Belize

Belizean Banyan Resort - Owner's Office

"I meant to ask you," D.J. said as he walked into Sione's office. "Did you talk to your dad about his visit to Moana?"

"Not quite sure where my dad is these days," Sione said, grabbing several loose sheets of paper to stack, trying to avoid his cousin's searching gaze. "Anyway, did you find out anything else about the situation with Spencer?"

"So, she's Spencer now?" D.J. smirked. "Well, according to one of my contacts, a body was found on Ambergris Caye," D.J. said, leaning back in the chair positioned in front of Sione's desk. "It was missing a hand."

"Was it Maxine Porter?"

"Body hasn't been identified," D.J. said. "But that's what I'm thinking. Oh, and I found out that Maxine Porter worked at Kwik Kash, too. At one time, she was the supervisor of Carla Garcia and

Karen Nelson."

"Did she have a criminal record?"

D.J. nodded. "Suspicion of money laundering."

"Money laundering?"

"Which is interesting," D.J. said. "Because about six months ago, Kwik Kash found itself under investigation by the Feds."

"What kind of investigation?" Sione asked.

"A multi-agency joint task force," D.J. said. "The FBI got in bed with the IRS to investigate predatory lenders. But as the task force looked into Kwik Kash, they realized the company was doing more than charging one thousand percent interest rates."

"Kwik Kash was suspected of money laundering?" Sione asked.

"And then it burned to the ground," D.J. said. "Along with a lot of business records and other items the federal government had subpoenaed but never received because they didn't survive the fire."

"Convenient," Sione said.

"Now, the interesting thing is," D.J. went on, "that I may have found a connection between the three women and Spencer."

Wary, Sione asked, "What kind of connection?"

"The manager of Kwik Kash where the three women worked was William Bermudez," D.J. said. "Bermudez is the guy who gave Spencer that gift."

"You think Bermudez told Spencer to deliver the money and fake passports to the three women?" Sione asked.

"It's possible," D.J. said. "Jared could ask Spencer about her connection to Bermudez. Of course, first you'd have to tell Jared what Spencer is up to."

"But I don't really know what she's up to," Sione said.

"Which is why you need to tell Jared about her," D.J. said. "So he can find out."

Sione glanced toward the windows that gave him an unrestricted view of the jungle. He knew D.J. was pissed at his hesitation. And he knew it was past time to get Jared involved. What Sione didn't know was the reason for his reluctance, but he had his suspicions, most of which he didn't want to admit—especially not to himself.

"You know, I'm starting to get the feeling that you're not interested in finding out the truth about Spencer," D.J. said. "You asked me to find out what she's trying to pull, and I've done that, but you couldn't give a shit, and you know why?"

Sione exhaled and then said, "I'm sure you'll tell me."

"Because I'm not telling you what you want to hear."

"What the hell do I want to hear?"

"You want me to tell you that Spencer is sweet and innocent," D.J. said. "You want me to tell you that she's being set up, or taken advantage of, by evil, nefarious people who mean to do her harm. You don't want me to tell you that she's a lying, scheming bitch, but I can't do that. Because she is a lying, scheming bitch."

"I know she's lied," Sione said.

"I don't have to waste time giving you evidence against this woman that you're just going to ignore," D.J. said. "I have other things I could be doing. I turned down several jobs to come here and help your ass."

"That's not true," Sione said. "You came down here because you needed the distraction. That's what Micah said. But I understand that. I could use a little distraction myself, especially right now."

"Why right now?" D.J. asked, and Sione suspected his cousin was glad for the chance to deflect and redirect the conversation away from his problems.

"All these issues with the land deal," Sione said, doing a bit of redirection himself, deciding to blame his need for distraction on the continued delays in securing land for his "guest tree houses" at the resort. "And speaking of that, I've got some proposals to go over."

D.J. got the message and after his cousin left, Sione found himself thinking about his cousin's initial question.

Did you talk to your dad about his visit to Moana?

A week ago, when D.J. had told him about Richard's visit to Moana, Sione had been harassed by the idea of going to see his father, and he couldn't shake the thought. Dealing with Richard was the last thing Sione wanted to do.

Ben's response to the reason Kelsey Thomas had been sent to search his casita had been ask your father. Sione had decided he didn't want to ask Richard anything and had told himself to forget about it. He didn't really care what Kelsey Thomas had been sent to find, what the hell his father had been looking for, or why his father thought it was somewhere in his casita.

Then Moana had called him, accusing Richard of wanting her dead.

Your father came to visit me in prison. He wanted me to steal something from Ben Chang.

Moana claimed she'd refused to fulfill Richard's request, but was that really true? Or had she convinced his cousin Peter to steal what Richard wanted?

An envelope that belonged to Ben Chang.

Peter had told him where the envelope was hidden, and Sione had confirmed that it was there, but he hadn't opened the envelope. He'd left it where Peter had stashed it.

Standing, Sione walked to the windows and stared out at the jungle. Since hearing Peter's story of the hidden envelope, Sione had been thinking about Kelsey Thomas. He'd caught her searching his casita office, and when confronted, she'd claimed to be looking for Sione's passport. Maybe she'd lied.

Supposedly, after finding the passport, she would get further instructions from Ben. The next steps. She'd claimed she had no idea what those next steps were. But, again, maybe she'd lied. Maybe Kelsey Thomas' next steps had something to do with what Richard had wanted Moana to steal from Ben Chang, which Sione assumed was the envelope Moana had told Peter to hide.

The idea of a connection between Kelsey Thomas and the hidden envelope was both taunting and teasing. Maybe Kelsey Thomas had been sent to retrieve the envelope Peter had hidden.

But, no, that didn't make sense.

Ben had sent Kelsey Thomas to look for something in his casita, but only because Richard had told Ben to send the woman on some scavenger hunt. Why would Richard tell Ben to have her search for an envelope that Richard wanted to steal from Ben?

Sione turned from the window and walked back to his desk. If he wanted answers, he would have to question his father. All roads led back to Richard. But those were dangerous roads, leading straight to hell. Roads he had to avoid, at all costs.

11

In the kitchen, Sione loaded plates and glasses in the dishwasher beneath the large island, feeling like a damn fool. Over veal and wine, he and Spencer had talked about a variety of things—mostly safe topics such as movies, books, television shows, and art.

Spencer hadn't been very forthcoming about her life back in Texas, which didn't surprise him, considering the painful memories she'd reluctantly shared with him. But she'd shared several entertaining, hilarious stories about her adventures with the girls, mimicking their voices and mannerisms and antics perfectly in her delivery.

Sione had talked about his life on the Pacific island of A'arotanga, where he'd lived for eight years, learning the real estate business from his uncle. He'd even told her about his ideas for the tree house expansion, giving her chapter and verse about all the highs and lows.

Not once had Sione brought up the fake passports and money.

While making dinner, he'd tried to decide how he would broach the subject with her and had figured he would just confront her. With no hesitation, or reservations, he would tell her that he knew she'd lied about the contents of the banker's box. And if she tried to deny his accusations, he'd tell her that DJ had found the Xanax box she'd delivered to Maxine Porter.

Dinner with her tonight was supposed to have been a good opportunity to demand answers, except he hadn't demanded answers. and he wasn't sure why. Maybe his reluctance had something to do with the very short skirt and the very revealing tank top she was wearing, but he couldn't blame his cowardice on her good looks.

Her beauty aside, he should have demanded to know what the hell was going on. He didn't know what his damn problem was when it came to Spencer. Yes, she was beautiful, but many girls looked just as good, and maybe even better, but whenever she came around, he lost focus, couldn't seem to concentrate, couldn't make sound decisions.

Disappointed in himself, Sione stacked more dirty plates into the dishwashing rack and then slammed the door. Taking a deep breath, he turned, catching sight of the refrigerator at the opposite end of the center island. On the door was the picture Spencer had been drawing when she suddenly burst into tears. Sione stared at the picture held in place by a magnet.

Spencer had been drawing palm trees and a blue sky and seemed to be outlining what might have been a boat in the ocean, if not for the long, incongruous pencil mark. The jagged line was like a scar against the paper, and for some reason, he thought of his own scars, the ones no one could see.

Little gashes and nicks kept hidden were always the deepest, most painful. Those emotional wounds had driven him halfway around the world to a place of swaying palms, blue skies, and turquoise water—a tranquil paradise where he'd began to heal.

Sione hadn't told Spencer the real reason he'd moved to A'arotanga. He'd made it sound like a well-thought out decision. The truth was, he'd fled there, escaping a brutal, violent destiny, the broad road leading straight to hell.

His uncle always said Sione had been snatched out of the fire. But "snatched out" meant he'd been in the fire, and he hadn't escaped unscathed—he'd been burned. He'd turned his life around, but he knew there was still an opportunity for the flames to flare up again, and it had almost happened with the Asian guy who'd attacked Spencer.

He'd been angry, and it had been so easy to abandon his progress and turn back to the old way of solving problems. For a split second, he could see his hand around the bastard's throat; he could see himself squeezing every breath from the man's body.

Sione shook the disturbing, depressing thoughts away, pissed that a stupid unfinished picture drawn by a crook could make him ruminate on things he liked to avoid. Exhaling, he turned.

Spencer stood in the arched entrance of the kitchen, staring straight ahead, almost transfixed, and when he followed her gaze, it led him to the refrigerator to the same unfinished, crudely drawn picture he'd been contemplating.

12

"What is that?" Spencer stared at the picture she'd been drawing with John's little second cousins, heart pounding as she focused on the crooked line trailing toward the edge of the paper.

In her mind, she'd imagined a tropical deserted island where a girl was all alone, but then she'd planned to add a man in a sailboat, maybe coming to rescue her, but she wasn't sure. She hadn't decided. Maybe he was coming to stay on the island with her. Maybe she would hit him in the head with a coconut, steal the boat, and leave him deserted.

"That's the picture you were drawing."

Spencer closed her eyes for a moment and then opened them. "Why is it on the refrigerator?"

"The girls wanted me to put it up there," he said. "They were hoping you would come back and finish it."

"I can't do that." She walked toward the refrigerator, thinking of how she'd always wanted to see the pictures she'd drawn as a child, proudly displayed, but that had never happened.

"Why not?" he asked.

Spencer looked at him, but his hazel eyes were too sincere again, and she had to look away. She didn't want to lie to him, but there was no other option. The truth was too painful, but it was her pain, exclusively for her, and she couldn't expect anyone else to understand it. She didn't even want anyone feeling sorry for her—especially not a man who would probably be the perfect hero, wrapping his strong arms around her while she cried.

She wasn't going to long for that kind of understanding and protection. She couldn't be weak and helpless. She wasn't going to start crying every time some bad memory showed up to torment her.

"Why didn't you finish the picture?" he asked. "Why'd you get so upset? You and my cousins were sitting there, having a good time, and then something happened, and—"

"Maggie asked me if I was going to give my picture to my mommy," Spencer snapped, frustrated and pissed by his damn questions. "And the answer was no, I would never give the picture to my mother, but I couldn't say that."

"Why not?"

"Because ..." She stopped, desperate to come up with some version of the truth that wouldn't reveal too much, that wouldn't leave her collapsed on the floor in tears. "Because my mother doesn't really like hand-drawn pictures, and ..."

John looked worried and too damn concerned. Spencer feared he was about to unleash another attack of questions she couldn't answer, questions she refused to answer, because she wasn't going to fall apart in front of him.

"Tell me why you got so upset that day?"

"Why do you have to know about that?" she asked, irritated. "Why does it matter why I got upset?"

"Because ..." John took her hand. "I want to know more about you, I want to understand you."

Sighing, she said, "Can't you ask me something else? I mean, I don't even really remember why—"

"Okay, then tell me why you don't want to tell me," he said.

Cursing softly, Spencer looked away, desperate to avoid the sadness that always accompanied memories of her mother's abuse, mistreatment, and neglect.

Shaking her head, she said, "I don't want to talk about it."

"Tell me," John coaxed.

Spencer glanced at him. The concern and compassion in his hazel eyes encouraged her, made her a little less apprehensive. "I got upset when Maggie asked me if I was going to give my drawing to my mother"—Spencer tried to keep her voice even and her emotions in check—"Because it made me remember this time when ..."

"When?"

Blinking, she looked away toward the wall of French windows that looked out toward the jungle. "My mother was angry and sad a lot." She cleared her throat. "She suffered from bipolar disorder. I realize that now, but when I was a little girl, I couldn't understand her mood swings, one minute she's happy and then she would get so furious."

"It's okay," John said. "You don't have to—"

"No, I do." She looked at him and then went on. "One time, when my mother was upset, I wanted to make her feel better. I decided to draw a picture of the two of us, holding hands, and ... she used to stay in her room with the door closed, and she would tell me not to bother her—"

"She told you not to bother her?"

"She just meant that she needed to rest." She was quick to

explain, hoping he wouldn't judge her mother too harshly. "Anyway, I knew I was supposed to let her rest, but I just wanted to show her the picture I'd made for her. I thought it might make her feel better, but …" As the tears welled and then slid down her cheeks, an overwhelming heaviness settled in Spencer's chest.

"Listen, it doesn't matter why you got upset," John said. "We don't have to talk about this right now—"

"I went into her room, and I told her I had drawn her a picture so she wouldn't be sad." She continued, unable to stop, even though the memories were brutal, almost killing her. "But she screamed at me, she told me that she needed to rest, and she couldn't understand why I couldn't just let her rest, and she said I was such a disappointment, and then she grabbed the drawing and ripped it to pieces, and she told me to go back to my room and to not come out until she told me to, and …"

Gently, John pulled her into his lap, wrapping his arms around her, and she tried to lose herself in his strong embrace, sobbing quietly as she remembered the rest of the story, the part she didn't want to tell him, the part that still terrified her.

As she'd watched the pieces of torn paper float to the ground, her mother screamed at her to get out and go back to her room. Eventually, she turned around and ran to her room. She'd closed the door and curled up in one of the corners, crying and trembling and confused, wondering what she had done wrong and wishing she could just disappear.

Moments later, her mother had entered her room. What happened next was still fuzzy in Spencer's mind. She only remembered the screaming curses and the excruciating pain. Then there was darkness. And then, light …

She'd opened her eyes to find her grandmother sitting next to her, clasping her hands as she whispered prayers, tears streaming down her cheeks. Much later, Spencer learned her mother had beaten her so severely, she'd suffered head trauma. Subsequently, she slipped into a coma and had woken up five days later.

A next-door neighbor had heard the terrifying commotion and called the police, but by the time the authorities had shown up, her mother had disappeared. She didn't return until five years later.

"I'm sorry," John said.

Sniffing, she lifted her head to look at him, knowing why he was sorry. John regretted asking her, regretted having to deal with another chapter from the book of her abusive, neglected childhood. Spencer regretted telling him. What the hell had she been thinking? What the hell was her damn problem? She had no right to share emotionally, gut-wrenching memories from her past with him. She had no right to act as though they were in some sort of relationship where the point was to get to know more about each other.

John wasn't some guy she was trying to build a life with. John was the man Ben had forced her to get close to, but not too close, so she could sneak around his casita looking for a damn envelope. She had to concentrate on getting the favor done. Then she could move on with her life.

It would be a life that didn't include John; a life that couldn't include him because they weren't right for each other. Good guys and bad girls only hooked up in those romance novels her sister Shady was always reading, and her life was not some romance novel.

Spencer didn't know what it was about the resort owner. Yes, he was handsome and sexy, very much so, but so were many guys. His muscles and good looks didn't give her license to forget she could go to jail if she didn't find the envelope.

Panicked by her wayward thoughts, Spencer put her arms around him. She would have to kiss him again, the way she had the last time they'd gotten too close to the topic of her mother. It was an incongruous act, considering the tension of her emotional turmoil, but kissing him was easier than struggling to think of some lie to steer him away from that painful subject.

She pressed her lips against his. He complied, but she sensed his reluctance and wasn't surprised when he removed her arms and broke the kiss, giving her a look she couldn't understand.

"I'm sorry." Embarrassed by her impulse, she slid off his lap and walked to the table, turning from his piercing gaze and trying to catch her breath. She'd only kissed him to distract him from the horrible story from her childhood, but kissing him was distracting in all the wrong ways. "Listen, I need to explain," she began and turned.

In the intervening moments, John had moved closer to her, eliminating the space and the strange tension that separated them. Their bodies were inches apart, and when she glanced up, the look in his hazel eyes was an intoxicating brew of desire and indignation.

Spurred by his gaze, without preamble or permission, Spencer stood on her toes, and this time John didn't hesitate to bend down so she could put her arms around him and press her mouth against his, letting her lips linger there, allowing the sensations to build and surge and float through her body. Feeling brazen, she parted his lips with her tongue, licking his bottom lip, pinching it softly between her teeth, giving it a few quick nibbles and gentle pecks before sliding her tongue deep into his mouth, circling her tongue around his. The kiss continued, unbroken, her hands moving over his muscles, along his pecs, and down his abs while their tongues swirl slowly.

Spencer felt John's fingers against her neck, moving over her collarbone. He touched her left breast, his index finger circling the swollen nipple, and then he broke the kiss, bending his head toward her neck, his mouth following the trail his fingers made.

Still in brazen mode, Spencer grabbed his other hand and led it beneath the hem of her flowing, gauzy miniskirt, pressing his hand against her leg. Taking her lead, John moved his hand along the inside of her thigh. His other hand was busy pulling the thin strap of her tank top off her shoulder, exposing her breast. Dipping his head lower, his mouth hovered over her nipple, his breath warm.

Spencer's heart slammed, and she bit her lip, the anticipation building between her legs, and when he pulled the crotch of her panties to the side and slid his finger near the opening of her vagina, she moaned, marveling at the pleasure of such a hesitant touch, so concentrated and searing.

Abruptly, John removed his fingers to untie his sarong, letting it fall to the floor. Spencer looked down at him, and her gasp was so loud, it was almost a scream. Was that a penis or a damn python? She half-expected a forked tongue to slither out of the head, and she imagined that when he put it in her, she'd feel it licking the inside of her walls as its huge thickness moved within her. Probably, as soon as he put it in, she'd feel the head teasing her cervix.

For a moment, they just stared at each other, and Spencer found herself thinking of practical matters. How did he walk with that damn elephant trunk? How did he sit? Go about his day? She was being facetious, ridiculous. It wasn't an elephant trunk or a python, but it was big. Huge. Long and thick. Her cousin Rusty would say a two by four. As pathetic and helpless and weak as it made her feel, she wanted it in her.

Eyes dark with lust, John grabbed her around the waist and lifted her from the ground. She wrapped her arms around his shoulder and her legs around his waist, shivering in anticipation. Moments later, he lowered her, and she felt him sliding inside her, huge, thick, swollen, and throbbing, taking her breath away. Holding on to her waist, his legs hip width apart and his feet planted firmly on the ceramic tile floor, he lifted her up and down his long, thick shaft. He stretched her, filling her so completely, she was practically screaming with the pleasure of it, grinding her hips with each powerful, vertical thrust.

Clutching her ass, he lifted her up and then moved her down on his penis, again and again, fast, then slow, then excruciatingly slow, and then fast again. She struggled to hold on as he moved her faster. She locked her legs around his waist, digging her heels into his lower back, groaning as she felt the pleasure building, and then exploding, and she cried out, shuddering.

Clasping her hands behind his neck, Spencer arched her back, tilting her head, and stared at the ceiling, panting and moaning. She felt his mouth on her left breast, his tongue flicking the nipple as he continued moving her up and down. Each time he was inside her, she squeezed her muscles around him, holding him prisoner, loath to release him, desperate to keep him deep inside her forever, straining to luxuriate in the pleasure she could only get from him.

Lifting her up, he turned her body so she was facing away from him toward the table. Seconds later, she was on the table on her hands and knees, trying to brace herself as he entered her from behind, filling her to capacity, and then he pulled out and slid in again.

He thrust into her again, and the table legs scraped against the tile floor. He withdrew and entered, and soon he found a pace that had the sturdy mahogany table groaning, but not as loud as she was, especially when he found a way to slip a hand between her legs to circle a finger around her clit.

And for a moment, it was almost too many sensations at one time, and she didn't know if she wanted to prolong the feelings so she could savor them or if she wanted them to come quickly, so she could explode again and again. She heard a sharp clap and simultaneously felt a warm sting on her left butt cheek.

Startled, she looked over her shoulder at him. "Did you just?"

He gave her an adorable, sheepish smile, but then he withdrew, slapped her ass, and thrust deep again. Spencer cried out in shock and wanted to protest, but the thrust-slap combination was like a jolt of supercharged electric pleasure, right through her walls, and it wasn't long before she went over the edge again and went limp.

Gasping and shaking, she was aware of him pulling out of her, and then she felt an arm beneath her legs and realized he was carrying her.

In the bedroom, he headed for the California king, and seconds later, she was airborne for a moment. Bouncing down on the mattress, she rolled over onto her back. John was on his knees in the bed, advancing toward her, still breathtakingly huge and hard.

Exhausted, she was a bit nervous, unsure if she could take much more of him and that python between his legs, but he didn't come at her like Ben would, demanding that she stay wet and tight for him. John kissed her for a long time, as if he'd been waiting all his life to do it.

Finally, he dragged his mouth from hers to her neck, and his tongue trailed along her throat. She felt his teeth grazing her skin and then came a series of gentle bites along her neck. She grabbed him and started to guide him, but he grabbed her hand and pinned it over her head against the pillow.

He slid inside her, and the first thrusts were slow and shallow. He gazed at her, but soon, his eyes darkened and his rhythm increased. He put one of her legs around his waist and the other over his shoulder, and then he got down to business, thrusting hard and deep —he wasn't playing around. Spencer dug her nails into the small of his back, struggling to keep up, trying to match his pace, but he was too big, too overpowering.

Spencer gave up, letting him have his way with her as strange thoughts filtered through her mind, crazy thoughts inspired by his long, deep strokes. What if she was falling in love with John? What if she was already in love with him?

John changed his pace to slow and shallow, and she clutched him, lifting her hips to meet his thrusts as she slipped her tongue into his mouth.

The thought of being in love with John—the idea and the consequences—seemed almost heretical, blasphemous. As he went deeper into her, slow … and then slow again … and then quick, quick, she thought of some ballroom dance … what was it called?

Falling in love was against each and every one of her core beliefs. But what if she was in love with John? How would she know for sure? How could she possibly know? What were the signs? The symptoms? Spencer had never been in love and had never even entertained the thought. The thought of giving her heart away was always too daunting, too melodramatic, and too tedious.

Finally, he thrust deep one last time. Spencer felt herself being lifted up off the bed as John rose to his knees, bringing her with him as he shuddered, whispering her name, causing another orgasm to erupt within her. The spasm shook her until she went limp again, half-conscious and unaware of her surroundings.

13

San Ignacio, Belize

Belizean Banyan Resort - Owner's Casita

"Good morning." Huge, thick, and magnificent, wearing the sarong and nothing else, John smiled at her as he stood at the stove making pancakes.

There seemed to be so much of him. Spencer couldn't stop staring and couldn't help but admire his broad shoulders and the muscles in his back and triceps. He inspired all sorts of wild fantasies, making her wish ridiculous things like they were together because they loved each other and they would be together forever.

She couldn't stop thinking about their lovemaking last night and how he'd touched her and kissed her, as if it was the only thing in the world he wanted to do.

Spencer hadn't meant to make love with John. The feelings had taken control of her before she realized it, and then it had been too late to turn back. A desperate, uncontrollable lust had taken hold of her, had claimed her, and she'd given herself over to lasciviousness.

Feeling blindsided, Spencer wobbled into the kitchen, groggy, thunderstruck, and wearing the old, faded T-shirt John had given her to wear with her hair pulled back into a careless bun.

"How are you?" John asked, flipping the pancakes over in the skillet.

"Good morning," Spencer said, taking a seat at the kitchen table. "I'm okay, but I kept dreaming about thunder."

"Probably because there was a storm last night," John said.

"A storm?" Spencer laid her head on the table.

"It was pretty bad," John said, walking to the table and placing a plate in front of her piled with pancakes, eggs, bacon, French toast with whipped cream, and hash browns.

Spencer sat up. "What's all this?"

"Breakfast." John sat next to her.

"There is no way I can eat all of this," Spencer said, her mouth watering as she polished off two pieces of bacon while she grabbed a fork and dug into the hash browns.

"Of course not," John said, watching her, his smile sly.

Spencer cut a triangular wedge from the stack of pancakes and shoved it into her mouth.

"This is sooo good," Spencer said, taking a mouthful of eggs, a strange idea slipping into her mind, although it was less of an idea and more like a fantasy.

Spencer imagined herself making breakfast for John. Bacon and eggs. And then she would pour coffee into his mug. Like a wife would do. And if she were "that wife," she would serve the coffee in skimpy lingerie. She'd seen her mother do that, but her stepfather hadn't always appreciated her mother's efforts; once, he'd thrown the coffee at her mother, screaming that it had been too hot, and—

Her heart thudding, she shook her head, wondering how the memory had managed to slip into her head. She hadn't thought about her mother's disastrous third marriage in years. Why the hell was she thinking about it now?

"Glad you approve of the eggs," John said and joined her at the table. "Listen, I need to talk to you about something."

"What?" Her appetite diminishing, she grabbed a napkin and wiped her mouth, convinced he was about to tell her last night had been a horrible mistake and they never should have made love.

"Well, I wanted to ask you about—"

A shrill ring cut through the air. Spencer glanced toward the sound, realizing it was the phone mounted on the wall near the refrigerator.

"I'll get it." John got up from the table and walked to the phone.

Her heart pounding, Spencer reached for her glass of water, wondering what John wanted to ask her.

"Hey, what's going on?" John asked the caller.

Spencer stared out of the kitchen window, her back to John, thinking about the blue folder with the photos of her Mayan ruin excursion. She hoped John wasn't going to interrogate her about the contents of that banker's box. She should probably get a story together, though, just in case.

"What?" John asked, his voice rising in excitement. "Are you serious?"

Curious, Spencer turned.

"Yeah, yeah. I can't believe this," John said and then faced her, giving her a wide smile. "Yeah, I'll be right there. I'll meet you at my office. One hour. See you then."

Spencer asked, "What is it?"

"The land owners finally agreed to all the terms," he said. "That was my cousin Truman. I'm meeting him in an hour to finalize everything and sign all the paperwork."

Squealing in delight, Spencer ran into his arms and John grabbed her, scooping her up and spinning her around. Moments later, after John left to take a shower, Spencer stood in the kitchen, elated for him.

She was excited about the tree house expansion and anxious to see John's visions and dreams come to life. John deserved to prove that he could make the resort profitable. He'd told her his Tuiali'i cousins didn't believe in him and secretly wanted him to fail. She was glad he would get to show them they were wrong about him.

More than anything, she was glad she wouldn't have to come up with some lie in response to whatever John was going to ask her about.

14

San Ignacio, Belize
Belizean Banyan Resort

"You don't know that the dead woman is Maxine Porter," Rae said.

"If it's not Maxine Porter's body, then who the hell is it?" Spencer demanded and jumped up from the chaise lounge near the pool. For the past two hours, she'd been clutching her cell phone, talking to her sisters about the newspaper article she'd read this morning. Four grim paragraphs detailed the discovery of a dead, partially decomposed body found in San Pedro.

It was a few minutes after five o'clock, and the pool was pretty much deserted, save for a few resort guests using it as part of a shortcut back to their casitas. Belize didn't participate in daylight savings time, and the sun was steadily sinking into the sky, dropping behind the jungle landscape.

"Maybe you should wait for a positive identification from the police," Shady suggested.

"I don't need a positive identification from the cops," Spencer said, pacing from the length of the chaise and back again. "The story said some tourists found the body of a dead woman and the right hand was missing. It's got to be the same right hand I found in Maxine Porter's closet. Those tourists found Maxine's body."

"You shouldn't jump to any conclusions before you know for sure," Shady said.

"While I'm trying to find out for sure, some psycho could be stalking me," Spencer said. "Planning to kill me and cut my hand off."

"Why do you think the person who killed Maxine would come after you?" Rae asked.

"Because I found her hand," Spencer said, rolling her eyes even though her sisters weren't there to appreciate her disdain.

"But how does her killer know you found the hand?" Shady asked. "You didn't go to the cops and tell them that you found it."

"I know, but …" Spencer trailed off, her thoughts scattered. "I just think I need to watch my back."

"Or maybe not," Rae said. "Ben Chang probably killed Maxine because of some shit that ain't got nothing to do with you. And you know Ben won't hurt you."

"You think he won't?"

Rae said, "You know how Ben feels about you."

"Yeah, I do," Spencer said. "He doesn't give a damn about me."

"That's not true," Shady said.

"Your ass would be in jail right now if he didn't care about you," Rae said.

"The only reason my ass is not in jail right now is because he is using me," Spencer said. "Trust me, he doesn't care about me. He just wants me to find that stupid envelope."

"I think Ben does care," Shady said. "But I don't think he killed

Maxine Porter. Why would Ben want money delivered to a woman he was planning to kill?"

"Her murder probably wasn't planned. Remember, Maxine called Spencer and said there was something wrong with the medicine," Rae said. "Obviously, what was wrong was that some of the cash Ben promised to give Maxine was missing. So, Maxine called Spencer to confront her. But, before Spencer showed up, Ben came to see Maxine. She confronted Ben about the missing money, so he killed the bitch and chopped her hand off."

"I think it was the guy with the green tattoo," Shady said. "What's his name? Tommy Wong?"

"Tommy Fong," Spencer corrected.

"That doesn't make sense," Rae said. "Why would Tommy Fong kill Maxine Porter? He probably didn't even know the woman."

"But Tommy Fong was in Maxine's condo," Shady pointed out.

"Because Fong followed Spencer there," Rae said. "Fong is after Spencer, not Maxine Porter."

"I don't think it was either one of them," Spencer said. "I think it was that guy Richard."

"Richard?" Shady asked.

"I told y'all about him." Spencer sank back down onto the cushions, moving beneath the wide umbrella covering the chaise. "Both Maxine and that blonde girl from the cave tour said they don't trust Richard. They both said he was the damn devil. They both said that if Richard found out they had gone against him, then Richard would kill them."

"But Richard whoever doesn't even know you," Rae said. "His beef is with Maxine and the blonde girl."

"Maybe he knows that I found the severed hand," Spencer said.

"How would he have found out?" Shady asked.

"I don't know!" Spencer snipped, rubbing her forehead. "I have to assume he did. Or he might. Which means he'll probably want me dead, too!"

"If you think that son of a bitch Richard is gonna come after you, then you need to leave Belize," Rae said.

"You can't stay there," Shady said. "And Ben will understand why you have to leave. Just tell him that—"

"Don't tell him shit," Rae said. "Think about yourself. Think about your life, okay? How the hell can you find that envelope Ben wants if your ass is dead?"

"How am I supposed to leave Belize without my passport?"

"You can get a new passport," Rae said.

Shady said, "It might take a few weeks, but—"

"Wait, that was the wrong question," Spencer said. "What I meant to ask was, how the hell can I leave Belize when I haven't found that damn envelope that Ben wants? Have y'all forgotten that if I don't find the envelope, then Ben will have me arrested, and the evidence he has against me will definitely put me in jail for a very long time?"

"No, we haven't forgotten," Shady said. "But—"

"Look, I can't leave Belize unless I find the envelope for Ben," Spencer snapped. "I can't get a new passport and get on a plane back to Texas, and I can't believe y'all would want me to do that knowing the kind of trouble I would be in!"

Exhaling in frustration, Spencer told her sisters she had to go and ended the call. Laying the cell phone on the chaise, Spencer dropped her face in her hands.

She shouldn't have gotten so pissed with her sisters. She shouldn't have allowed her fears and frustrations to get the best of her. Rae and Shady meant well. They were just worried about her. They hated the corner Ben had backed her into, and more than anything, they wanted this nightmare with Ben to be over. Spencer did too—more than ever. The damn envelope had to be found. There was no getting out of the favor she had to do.

"You okay?"

Spencer looked up, frantic as she swiped tears from her face.

John stared down at her, looking much too handsome in the fading sunlight, framed by a pink and lavender sky.

"Yeah, I'm fine," she said.

"You sure?" He sat on the chaise next to her.

"Not really," she said, staring at the water. "I mean, yes. I don't know. I just …"

"What?"

She turned to him. "Did you read in the newspaper about a dead body that was found by some tourists on Ambergris Caye?"

"No, I don't think I did."

Spencer took a breath and said, "It was Maxine Porter."

"That's what the newspaper said?"

"They didn't need to say it," Spencer said. "The dead body was missing a hand, John. And I know the missing hand is the same hand I found in Maxine Porter's closet."

"But we don't know that the hand you found was Maxine's," John said.

"Whose hand was it except Maxine's?" Spencer asked, her frustration increasing. "Before I got to her condo, somebody killed her and then cut her hand off and left it behind while they took her body and dumped it in the jungle. And what if the same thing happens to me?"

"Why do you think the person who killed Maxine would come after you?"

"Because maybe …" Spencer looked at her toes. "Maxine's killer might know that I found her severed hand."

"Listen, nobody knows that you were at Maxine Porter's condo that day," John said. "My cousin took care of things. He made sure that the cops wouldn't have a reason to question either one of us about the situation. He made it look like we were never there."

Confused, Spencer asked, "Why did he do that?"

"Because he didn't want me associated, in any way, with a hand that had been chopped off and left in a closet," John said. "We both thought it would be bad for the land deal. Which probably wasn't the right thing to do. We should have gone to the cops. But there wasn't really anything we could tell them. I didn't know Maxine. And neither did you, right?"

"No, I didn't know her," Spencer said, then stood, and walked to the edge of the pool. She hadn't really told John a lie, but she still wasn't being entirely honest with him.

"You don't know what she was involved in," John said. "You don't know who she was involved with."

Spencer stared at the water, knowing she couldn't tell John the truth. She knew exactly who and what Maxine Porter had been involved with.

"Spencer ..."

After a deep breath, she turned and took a step toward him, feeling a bit desperate.

"I'm not going to let anyone hurt you, okay?" John took a step toward her. "So, don't worry."

"How can I not worry?" she asked. "A woman was killed and her hand was cut off, for whatever sick, twisted reason, and I found the hand and—"

"Trust me," he said, pulling her closer to him, gazing at her with those beautiful hazel eyes. "I will keep you safe."

Spencer stared up at him, anxious to give in to him even as she told herself to hesitate. It wouldn't be good to be too eager, to give him the power of knowing she needed him to be the hero for her right now.

She needed him to be her hero forever.

A few minutes passed, then Spencer stepped into his arms, and as he embraced her, she held on to him for dear life.

15

"Micah says Ms. Edwards is living with you now?" D.J. walked into Sione's office, closing the door behind him.

Sione glanced up from the cost analysis reports he'd been reviewing and exhaled. His cousin's question held an insinuation Sione didn't want to deal with, not after the long, demanding day he'd endured, starting with a nine o'clock meeting with Truman and the owners of the construction company he was thinking about hiring to build the tree houses.

"Is that true?" D.J. asked and dropped down in the chair in front of Sione's desk.

"Only because I was having extra surveillance cameras installed around the honeymoon casita," Sione said, defensive, pissed that he felt the need to explain his decisions to his cousin. "And because there's still a chance the Asian guy might come after her again."

D.J. gave him a dubious side-eye and asked, "How long has she been staying with you?"

Shrugging, Sione said, "Just a few days."

"Aunt Carmen says she babysits Terry's girls," D.J. said. "Is that true?"

"They like her," Sione said, thinking of all the times he'd gone back to the casita for lunch and had found Spencer with the girls—or the sprites, as she called them—dancing around, coloring, doing each other's nails, or some other girly stuff with makeup. "And she loves them."

Frowning, obviously disappointed, D.J. said, "So, let me get this straight. Ms. Edwards is living with you. She calls you John—"

"It's my name." Sione glared at him. "Sione means John."

"She babysits our cousins," D.J. went on. "And, according to Micah, the two of you sleep in the same bed every night."

Grabbing his coffee, Sione shrugged. "So what?"

D.J. smiled. "Your situation seems rather domesticated."

Sione didn't really know what the situation was or how to define what was happening between him and Spencer. It was some sort of gray area and unprecedented, unlike any other relationship he'd had with a woman. But he liked it and hoped it wouldn't end, at least not anytime soon.

"Tell me something." D.J. leaned forward. "Did she lie to you? Or did she come clean?"

"What are you talking about?"

"You were going to tell her you knew the truth about the Xanax boxes," D.J. said. "And then you were going to ask her what was really going on. So, have you done that?"

Sione glanced at the financial reports on his desk. Spencer's fears about the dead body found on Ambergris Caye would have been the perfect time to confess his knowledge about the Xanax boxes. But days had passed, and Sione still hadn't carried out his plan to find out whether or not Spencer would be honest with him about the contents of the banker's box she'd received.

"I didn't think so."

"I've been busy," Sione said defensively. "We got the land deal done. Finally. I'm starting to review construction bids, so—"

"You haven't asked her because you don't want to know the answer."

Sione shook his head. "That's not true."

"It is true, and you know it," D.J. accused. "You are falling for this shady bitch, and you don't want to know the truth."

"She's not a shady bitch. And I haven't asked because I don't think it matters—"

"This woman delivered fake passports and money and it doesn't matter?"

"Whatever her part was, she played it, and her involvement in it is finished," Sione said.

"You know what your problem is?"

Exhaling, Sione rubbed his jaw.

"You're afraid that all your suspicions about her will come true," D.J. said. "You know you should stay away from her. You know she's a liar, but you don't care because you're in love with her."

"That's not true," Sione disputed, leaning back in his chair.

He liked Spencer and wanted to know if something more could develop between them. But he wasn't in love. At least, he didn't think he was …

"Anyway, the reason I stopped by is that I found out the San Pedro cops positively identified the dead body they found a few days ago," D.J. said. "I was right. It was Maxine Porter."

Dragging a hand along his jaw, Sione said nothing. He wasn't surprised at the news, but the confirmation still bothered him.

"I wanted to talk to Ms. Porter about that Xanax box Ms. Edwards gave her," D.J. said. "But, of course, I can't ask her. So, I'll have to ask someone else."

Apprehensive, Sione asked, "Who?"

"You'll see …"

16

San Ignacio, Belize
Black Orchid Inn

It definitely was a sign, Sione thought, staring at the "Do not disturb" sign on the door. They weren't supposed to be there.

"We should go," Sione said, kicking himself for letting D.J. pressure him into taking what his cousin referred to as a "field trip" to the Black Orchid Inn.

Housed in a colonial building showing signs of wear and tear, the Black Orchid Inn was a three-star bargain establishment. It catered to budget-conscious travelers who didn't need a lot of frills and fancy amenities and only wanted a decent bed to sleep in after a long day of back-to-back excursions.

The Black Orchid Inn was where Carla Garcia, the girl in the yellow visor, had booked room 442.

"We just got here," D.J. said.

"She doesn't want to be disturbed." Sione pointed to the sign and looked left and then right down the long hallway, which smelled like stale smoke and pine cleaner. The atmosphere in the building was slightly damp, suggesting a mold and mildew problem.

"We won't take up much of her time," D.J. said, knocking on the door. "We only have a few questions."

Sione knew the questions D.J. wanted to pose to Carla Garcia. Questions he really didn't want to know the answers to. Questions with answers that might be a direct indictment against Spencer.

"She's not answering," Sione said. "Maybe she's sleeping."

D.J. knocked a bit more forcefully.

"Or maybe she checked out."

"She didn't check out."

"How do you know?" Sione asked, looking left, toward the door to the EXIT stairwell at the end of the hall.

"Friends," D.J. said and pounded his fist against the door.

"We need to go," Sione said, worried about the security cameras. "She's not going to open the door."

"I think you're right," D.J. conceded. "We'll have to surprise her."

"Surprise her?" Sione's pulse jumped. "What the hell do you mean?"

D.J. reached into the front pocket of his Levi's and pulled out what looked like a key card.

"Is that what I think it is?"

D.J. nodded and slipped the card into the entry slot on the door. "It is."

"How the hell did you get that?"

"Friends," said D.J., then pushed the door lever down, and opened the door.

"Wait a minute." Sione stretched an arm in front of the doorway, blocking D.J. "If we go into this hotel room, we'll be breaking the law."

"Delivering fake passports is against the law, too," D.J. said. "But you don't seem to have a problem with that."

Glaring at his cousin, Sione withdrew his arm.

"Well, well, well," D.J. said, after slipping behind the door. "Looks like the surprise is on us."

Stepping into the tiny entryway, Sione let the door close behind him as he scanned Carla Garcia's small room. Late afternoon sunlight flooded the room, a hazy golden spotlight on the destruction and disarray. The place looked as though a bomb had gone off in it.

The bed was in shambles. The duvet and sheets were strewn across a mattress, which had been stripped bare, then flipped up, and leaned against the headboard. There were clothes all over the floor. The desk in the corner had been knocked over, and the accompanying chair had been turned upside down. All six of the bureau drawers had been pulled out. Two framed photographs, black orchids shot in black-and-white, lay on the floor, the frames broken, the glass shattered. A lamp had been smashed and left in pieces in front of a bedside table.

"What the hell?"

"Looks as though someone made a frenzied, chaotic search for something in Ms. Garcia's room," D.J. said, walking to the window and pulling back the drapes. "I'll check the closet and the bathroom. You look around in here."

"What the hell am I looking for?" Sione asked, confused, feeling as disheveled as the room appeared.

While D.J. opened the accordion doors to the closet and peeked inside, Sione made his way around to the other side of the bed. Hesitating, he picked up the duvet and bed linens from the floor. A small gecko scurried across the stained pile carpet. Cursing under his breath, he dropped the linens on the exposed box spring. He didn't want to look for anything.

He didn't want to figure anything out. He didn't want to speculate. He didn't want to try to make sense of why Carla Garcia's hotel room had been ransacked. He didn't care what the culprit had been searching for.

He just wanted to get the hell out of room 442 and away from the Black Orchid Inn. He wanted to get back to the Belizean Banyan, back to the invoices and the payroll and all the other mindless administrative tasks that distracted him and kept his mind off things he didn't want to think about.

"Jackpot!" D.J. called out. "Take a look inside."

Sione turned, just in time to catch the pink beach bag his cousin pitched toward him. Recognizing the Belizean Banyan logo on the bag, his heart raced. Remembering the photo of Spencer holding the pink bag, he opened it. Inside were bundles of money and a passport.

Sione's speeding heart dropped into his stomach. He felt himself careening toward a conclusion he didn't want to deal with. Whoever had trashed the hotel room had been looking for something, but not the Xanax box.

The fake passport and money had been left behind.

Despite the way Carla Garcia's hotel room had been tossed, it wasn't the work of some robber. Whoever had broken in hadn't been looking for some*thing*. They'd wanted to find some*one*. Carla Garcia.

It wasn't a stretch to conclude that the person looking for Carla Garcia had first gone hunting for Maxine Porter. Someone who hadn't been interested in the fake passport and money, but instead had killed Maxine Porter, chopped off her hand, and left it behind.

Sione reached into the bag, took out the passport, and opened it. The name was RIVERA, ANNA, and the thumbnail photo was of the dark-haired Hispanic woman.

"We have a problem ..." D.J. called from the bathroom.

Sione dropped the passport back into the beach bag, tossed it on the box spring, and headed into the bathroom. "What is it?"

"Take a look in the bathtub," D.J. said and stepped aside so Sione could enter.

Apprehensive, Sione stared at his cousin. "What the hell am I going to be looking at?"

"Nothing you haven't seen before."

Sione went into the bathroom and looked down into the tub.

A severed hand.

Cursing, he stared at the small, dismembered appendage, tiny and delicate, blood coating the stiff fingers. A clean chop from the wrist, just like the hand found in Maxine Porter's condo.

"A right hand," D.J. said. "I'm thinking female. And I'm also thinking you should tell Jared about Spencer's connection to Maxine Porter, Carla Garcia, and Karen Nelson."

Sione took a deep breath, trying to focus and put things in perspective. The right thing to do would be to tell Jared what he knew—and not just what he knew about Spencer's deliveries to the three women. He should tell Jared his suspicions about who had killed Maxine Porter, which were more than just suspicions. He was certain he knew who'd left the severed hand in Maxine Porter's closet. But if he told Jared, his cousin would ask a whole lot of damn questions, and Sione didn't have any answers to give him. Not any truthful answers, anyway.

"We don't know that Spencer and those women have a connection," Sione said.

D.J. said, "We know that Spencer delivered money and a fake passport to both of those women."

"Spencer made the deliveries," Sione said. "But she doesn't know either of those women. Why do I need to tell Jared about a connection that probably doesn't even exist."

"I don't understand you," D.J. said. "Why the hell are you protecting this woman?"

Sione looked away for a moment and then back at his cousin. "I'm not protecting Spencer."

"Spencer Edwards is bad news, and you know it," D.J. said. "But, still, you crawl into bed every night with a woman who probably knows who killed Maxine Porter and Carla Garcia."

Sione shook his head, trying to control his anger. Every word out of D.J.'s mouth since he'd opened it had pissed him off, but when his cousin had used the phrase *crawl into bed every night,* Sione wanted to put him in a damn chokehold.

The words suggested a lurid, physical relationship that didn't exist. He and Spencer shared a bed, and they made love in it, but they didn't have mindless, meaningless sex. And he wasn't interested in inconsequential lovemaking. Sione wanted things to be different between them.

"We don't know that Carla Garcia is dead," Sione said.

"I'm sure that's her hand in that shower," D.J. said, jerking his thumb toward the bathroom. "And I'm sure the cops will find her body dumped somewhere. What I'm not sure is why you want to be with a woman who associates with people that deal in fake passports and cut off women's hands after they kill them?"

Sione glared at his cousin. "You know what your damn problem is?"

With a mirthless laugh, D.J. said, "I get the feeling you're gonna try to tell me."

"The only reason you don't trust Spencer is because you just don't trust women."

Shaking his head, D.J. gave him an incredulous glare.

"You're suspicious of all women," Sione said, "because of what's going on with you and your wife. Micah told me you're getting a divorce."

D.J. scowled, his arms crossed. "That's none of your damn business."

"And my relationship with Spencer—"

"Oh, you're in a relationship with her, now?"

"—is none of your damn business," Sione said, stepping closer to D.J., getting in his face, itching to put his fist in the center of it. "But you listened pretty intently when Micah told you that I *crawl into bed* with her every night. But he couldn't tell you why because I didn't tell him that I am only trying to keep her safe. I'm trying to make sure she doesn't end up like Maxine Porter or Carla Garcia!"

"If you really want to keep her safe," D.J. said, "then tell her what you know about the Xanax boxes and convince her to come clean to Jared."

17

San Ignacio, Belize

Belizean Banyan Resort - Owner's Casita

With a cup of coffee, Spencer sank down into the Banyan wood rocking chair on the wide porch in front of John's casita. This morning, after she and John had made love, after the last kiss and the last shuddering release, guilt and apprehension had plagued Spencer as she remembered *Step Three*. Cocooned in John's arms, peace eluded her. All she could think about was finding that damn envelope so she could move on with her life.

A new life with John maybe—hopefully. A life where they would develop a morning routine of early morning lovemaking and then a hearty breakfast. They would talk about their plans for the day and discuss the tree house expansion, which Spencer never tired of hearing about and was anxious to see implemented. Then John would head off to work. She would walk him out to the porch, give him a kiss, and watch him head off down the path toward the administration building. When he was finally out of sight, Spencer would sink into the rocking chair and allow herself the luxury of enjoying the jungle.

Setting the coffee mug on the small table next to the chair, Spencer sighed. She had to let go of this silly fantasy about this new life with John, a life where they had met under different circumstances. She couldn't pretend she hadn't met John because of the favor she had to do for Ben Chang.

The favor would always intrude on her solitude, hanging over her happiness like a dark cloud. Her time with John had been, so far, wonderful, but she was wary of becoming complacent.

Life was like one of those beautiful, sunny days when all she could see stretched before her was blue skies and fluffy white clouds ... and then she would look over her shoulder and see those large, looming thunderclouds. Foreboding and ominous, they seemed far away, tricking her into thinking there was enough time to bask in the sun. Too soon, the rain would come.

Weary and disillusioned, Spencer headed back into the casita to look for the damn envelope.

Thirty minutes later, she stood in the middle of a small study, a mahogany-paneled room lined with bookshelves, her gaze roaming from the desk at the back of the room to the couch in front of the desk to the chair in the corner.

The first bedroom on the second wing of guest rooms she'd searched had been a bust, and she wasn't holding out any hope of finding anything in the study. Fighting panic, Spencer dropped down onto the chair in the corner, trying to summon the will or the guts or whatever the hell she needed to continue the search.

One last bedroom, and then the living room, the den and the library. Four more rooms to search. Four more chances to find the envelope. What if she didn't? What the hell was she going to do?

Start the search all over again? Ben was convinced the envelope was in John's casita. What if it wasn't?

She would never be able to convince Ben that she hadn't found the envelope because it wasn't in the casita. Ben would assume she hadn't looked long enough or hard enough; he'd accuse her of trying to escape the consequences of her mistakes, and then—

He would burn her grandmother's house down.

She rose from the chair, picked up the accent pillow, and tossed it over onto the couch. Just as she had with the couch, Spencer lifted the bottom cushion seat.

Her heart shot into her throat and she started to tremble.

A lambskin envelope sealed with a dragon wax stamp.

Struggling to catch her breath, Spencer could hardly believe what she was staring at.

It was the envelope Ben wanted.

She'd found it.

18

"So, I'm guessing you haven't found out if Spencer is going to come clean about her involvement with the Xanax deliveries, have you?" D.J. asked, though it was more of an accusation, or an indictment, than a question.

Sione turned from his computer to stare at his cousin, who'd waltzed right into his office without knocking or allowing Marie to announce him.

"I've been busy," Sione said, though he couldn't even remember how long ago it had been since he'd told D.J. he would confess his knowledge about the Xanax boxes in an effort to garner a confession from Spencer.

"Yeah, busy trying to convince yourself that Spencer isn't a lying bitch."

"Is there a reason why you're here?" Sione asked.

"Actually, there is," D.J. said. "Not that I think you'll do anything positive or productive with the information I'm about to give you, like share it with Jared, but I'm going to tell you anyway, and you can let your conscience be your guide."

"What information?"

"Maxine Porter, Carla Garcia, and Karen Nelson all have more in common with each other beside the fact that they each received a fake passport and money from Ms. Edwards," D.J. started. "Remember I told you they worked together at Kwik Kash? And then I told you that Kwik Kash came under investigation for money laundering?"

"Yeah," Sione said.

"The women also found themselves under investigation by the Feds," D.J. said. "They were offered a deal. Immunity in exchange for ratting out the real owner of Kwik Kash—which was something the Feds didn't know and were having a hell of a hard time figuring out."

"Okay, yeah, so," Sione said.

"Once the three women came under investigation, I think the owner of Kwik Kash got wind of things and told the ladies to skedaddle. The owner paid the women not to testify against him. And he arranged for them to get passports under new names, probably so they could leave the country and become new people."

"That's possible," Sione said, wary. He had a feeling his cousin was dragging out the story on purpose, working his way toward some shocking, or unexpected, revelation.

"Now, if you'll remember," D.J. went on. "I told you that Maxine Porter, Carla Garcia, and Karen Nelson all worked together at Kwik Kash, and their manager was William Bermudez, the guy who gave Ms. Edwards that gift she didn't seem too happy to receive."

Sione nodded, his apprehension increasing. "We'd figured

Bermudez was the guy Spencer was supposed to contact when she got to Belize."

"Bermudez probably gave Spencer instructions about delivering the fake passports and money," D.J. said. "But who told Bermudez to give Spencer those instructions."

"We don't know."

"We *didn't* know," D.J. said, looking a bit too smug, in Sione's opinion. "But we do now."

Rubbing his chin, Sione waited, feeling the need to prepare himself or brace himself.

"I told you the house that William Bermudez is renting is owned by Blue Mountain LLC," D.J. said. "Well, interestingly enough, Maxine Porter's condo is also owned by Blue Mountain LLC."

"That is interesting."

"Blue Mountain LLC, is a subsidiary of The Leviathan Group, which is a holding company of another company called Borrowed Lizard Enterprises," D.J. said.

"Borrowed Lizard?" Sione asked.

"Blue Mountain LLC owns Kwik Kash also," D.J. said. "I had to peel back a lot of layers to find out the owner of Blue Mountain LLC, and it took me a while. But eventually, I found out that Borrowed Lizard Enterprises, which owns The Leviathan Group, which owns Blue Mountain LLC, which owns Kwik Kash, William Bermudez's house, and Maxine Porter's condo, is owned by … Ben Chang …"

Sione stared at his cousin, waiting for some kind of punch line, but D.J. just stared at him.

"While you struggle to process that information," D.J. said. "I will tell you my new theory, which is that Ben arranged for the women to get new identities and gave them money so they wouldn't be convinced to testify against him. And I think Ben told Ms. Edwards to make those deliveries for him. Which means, Ms. Edwards is connected to Ben Chang."

"I don't believe that," Sione said, his heart pounding as he turned back to his computer.

"What don't you believe?" D.J. asked.

Sione stared at the screen, still trying to wrap his mind around D.J.'s latest bombshell, even though he knew he couldn't. He would never be able to come to terms with what D.J. was trying to make him believe.

"Spencer is not working for Ben Chang." Sione shook his head and then faced his cousin. "It's not true."

D.J. leaned forward. "Then what is the truth about that damn woman?"

"I don't know."

"Don't you think it's time to find out?" D.J. asked. "Don't you think it's time to have a long, serious conversation with Spencer Edwards?"

19

———————

San Ignacio, Belize
Belizean Banyan Resort - Owner's Casita

Another day had begun, and once again, Sione was waking up with Spencer in his arms. As they whispered their good mornings, he was enticed and addicted by the hypnotic feeling of her lush curves pressed against him, reminding him of last night's lovemaking.

Since she'd moved into the casita, Sione now looked forward to closing his eyes every night with her arms wrapped around his waist and her legs entwined with his.

Every morning, they had breakfast, talking and fooling around, and then she would give him a kiss before he went off to work. That sensuous peck on the lips would carry him through his day, and he would think of her as he headed into his meetings and dealt with guest issues or other problems. That kiss was her promise to him that she would be there when he came home, waiting to kiss him again as he walked through the door.

He was hoping she would stay in Belize and see what might happen between them, but …

As much as Sione liked having her in his life, he was still bothered by the idea of some connection between her and Ben Chang. No, he was more than bothered by the idea. He was pissed and worried and disappointed.

Ben had tricked him with Kelsey Thomas, sending the woman to search through his home on some strange, secret errand for Richard.

And yet, Sione had gotten past the anger—or so he'd told himself. But finding out Ben was the owner of Kwik Kash, and had been behind the scenes, orchestrating Spencer's every move, had reignited the animosity he felt toward Ben.

The hatred Sione believed would never subside had flared up again. Ben's constant acts of betrayal and vengeance would probably never end. It would always be war between them.

The battles had begun when they were sixteen, too young to really understand what they had set in motion that hot, humid night when Sione had failed to live up to Richard's expectations. Since that night, Ben had usually been the first to strike, always a devastating wound, worse than fatal. A mortal wound would end in death. What Ben inflicted would last a lifetime, a bloody, gaping gash that would never really heal.

"I'm going to take a shower," Spencer said, kissing him. "You gonna join me?"

"Yeah." He smiled at her. "But first, I need to talk to you about something."

She started to move away from him, but Sione stopped her, pulling her back toward him.

"What is it?" Spencer asked, a trace of worry in her gaze.

The same worry snaked through him, almost convincing him to save the conversation he wanted to have with her for another time, like maybe never. It was a conversation they needed to have, even though it might ruin things between them, might stir up discord and mistrust and suspicion. The last thing Sione wanted was to drive Spencer away.

He didn't want to wake up alone anymore.

But after his talk with D.J., Sione knew he had to find out if Spencer would tell him the truth about the fake passports and money she'd delivered.

"John?" she prompted, her voice holding traces of curiosity and anxiousness.

He tightened his hold on her, and as she relaxed against him, her cheek resting on his chest, he wished they could just stay in bed all day. "I want to ask you something," he started. "And I want you to be honest with me."

"You say that like you don't think I would be honest with you."

Sione wasn't sure if she would be honest or not. But if she did lie to him, he hoped it wouldn't be to purposely deceive him for her own selfish gain, but maybe to avoid disappointing him. Or maybe she would lie to protect what was happening between them, because she didn't want the relationship to end before it really began.

"Well, first, I need to be honest with you about something," he said. "And I guess I'm hoping that if I'm honest and if I come clean with you, then you will be honest and come clean with me."

"What do you need to be honest and come clean with me about?" she asked.

"About the banker's box," he said. "I opened it. I know that you were not expecting training manuals. I know what was really in the box. I know what was hidden in the Xanax boxes."

Sione felt her body tense, but he went on and said, "I know that there were three Xanax boxes, and inside each box was a passport and a whole lot of money."

Spencer moved away from him and sat up, pulling the bed linens over her breasts.

Sione sat up. "I know you delivered the money and passports to three different women. Carla Garcia, Karen Nelson, and Maxine Porter."

"How did you find out that I delivered the money and passports to those women?" she asked, putting more space between them.

"My cousin D.J.," Sione admitted. "When I found the money and passports, I called D.J. and told him to find out what was going on with you."

"So, you told your cousin to spy on me?"

"I just wanted D.J. to find out what was going on," Sione said. "You have to understand. When I saw all that money hidden in those Xanax boxes, I didn't know what to think. And I didn't want to call the cops because I didn't know why the money and passports had been delivered to you."

"Well, I guess now you know what's going on," she said. "Your cousin told you."

"I don't know everything. I don't know who told you to come to Belize and deliver the money and passports."

"Didn't your cousin find out?"

"I want you to tell me."

"I can't," she snapped. "Because I don't know."

"You don't know?"

"I never met the guy," she said. "That's the way I think he wanted it so if things didn't go as planned, and I got myself arrested or in worse trouble, I wouldn't be able to tell the cops anything about him."

"You don't know anything about him?" Sione asked, confused, not sure if he believed her, but not sure he was suspicious.

"All I know is that he owns the payday loan place where I went to about six months ago," she said. "I made the mistake of borrowing five thousand dollars. I didn't realize I was doing so at five hundred percent interest until I got the bill for twenty-five thousand dollars. There was no way I could pay that. Honestly, I couldn't even pay back the five thousand."

"Why did you borrow the money?"

"I lost my job. I couldn't find a new one," she said. "My credit cards were maxed out. I was barely paying the minimum on them. The five thousand dollars was to pay my rent and my car note for another three months.

"Anyway, when I went back to the loan store, I asked to speak with the owner," she said. "I was told that I would not be able to meet the owner because the owner didn't live in Houston. I was told the owner lived in Jamaica. So, I gave my sad story to the manager, and I asked him to please relay it to the owner. I was hoping the owner would be willing to work with me and give me some extra time to pay back the loan. Well, a week later, I got a call from the loan manager, and he wanted to meet with me. The loan manager had relayed my story to the owner, and the owner thought there was a way that he could help me."

"How did the owner say he would help you?" Sione asked, waiting for an explanation, hoping it was something he could believe.

"The owner made me an offer I didn't think I could refuse," Spencer said. "He would forgive the entire loan if I did him a favor which was to come to Belize and deliver money and a passport to those three women. But if I didn't do the favor, then the loan manager sort of let me know, without coming out and saying it, that the owner would make my life hell."

"And the owner didn't tell you why he wanted money and a passport delivered to those women?"

"No, because I never met the owner," she said. "I don't even know what his name is. I know the orders were coming from him, but the loan manager was telling me what the owner wanted me to do. The owner and I never met face to face."

"Did the loan manager tell you why the owner wanted money and passports delivered to the women?"

Spencer shook her head. "And I didn't ask."

"Probably best that you didn't," Sione said. "If the owner is who I think he is—"

"Who do you think he is?"

Sione sighed, rubbing his jaw. "His name is Ben Chang."

"Ben Chang?" Spencer stared at him, a few emotions flickering in her brown eyes—surprise, and a few others he didn't really recognize —that made him think she was worried about something.

"D.J. found out that Carla Garcia, Karen Nelson, and Maxine Porter worked together at a payday loan business in Houston," he said. "It was called Kwik Kash, and it was owned by Ben Chang."

"Kwik Kash is the name of the place I went to."

"D.J. told me Ben Chang owns several Kwik Kash businesses in the states," Sione said. "So, Ben Chang is the anonymous owner who sent you to Belize to make those deliveries."

"So, this Ben Chang guy," Spencer started. "Is he dangerous? Because you said it was best that I didn't ask why he wanted money and fake passports delivered to Carla, Karen, and Maxine."

"He's more than dangerous," Sione said. "He's a crazy, cold-blooded sonofabitch ..."

Sione grabbed the back of his neck, massaging it as he stared at the footboard.

He needed to calm down and get himself together, but it was hard. It was always damn near impossible to control his anger when it came to Ben Chang and the history they shared, the bloody past he always tried to forget, that he'd barely escaped.

"How do you know he's dangerous?"

Staring at her, Sione was relieved to see only concern, and no suspicion, on her face. It was risky, presenting the information about Ben to her as though, like her, he'd never met the man. He felt like a hypocrite, trying to find out if she knew Ben when he wasn't willing to admit his own connection to the bastard.

"Dangerous *how* is what I meant," Spencer said, staring at him, like she wasn't sure what to say. "Do you think Ben Chang could have killed Maxine Porter?"

"I wouldn't put it past him," Sione said, though he wasn't exactly sure. "But I want you to know this—I'm not going to let Ben Chang hurt you."

"John, you don't have to—"

"Yes, I do," he said, pulling her back into his arms. "If Ben tries to hurt you, I will kill him."

"Don't say that," Spencer said, resting her hand against his jaw. "I don't want you to kill anybody because of me! It's my own fault that I got involved in delivering money and fake passports, you can't—"

"Listen to me," Sione said, holding her face in his hands as he stared at her. "I'm going to keep you safe from that bastard. I promise. I'm not going to let anything bad happen to you."

20

San Ignacio, Belize

Belizean Banyan Resort - Owner's Office

Sione played the recorded voice message again. For the fourth time. The message had consumed his attention from the first time he'd heard it, and as much as he wanted to ignore it, to erase it and move on with his life, he didn't think he'd be able to.

"You don't know me, but I really need to talk to you." The woman's voice was a tense, rushed whisper, as though she only had one chance to leave the message and she had to be clear and convincing. "My name is Karen Nelson."

Karen Nelson.

Sione knew the name. D.J. had told him all about Karen Nelson. Her image from the fake passport came to him along with the surveillance photos D.J. had snapped of her during the cave exploration excursion. A freckle-faced blonde.

"I need to talk to you about Maxine Porter and Carla Garcia," she said. "Can you please meet me? I don't want to talk over the phone."

The message continued with Karen Nelson's furtive whispering, telling him where she was staying, giving him the exact address, and promising to be there later this evening around six o'clock.

"I know you have no reason to believe me, but ..." She trailed off for a few seconds and then said, "I really need to tell you what I know."

The message ended.

Again, for the fourth time, Sione sat back in the leather chair, confused and wary. He wasn't sure what to do or whether to believe Karen Nelson's frantic murmurings.

After listening to the message the first time, Sione had wondered why had Karen Nelson decided to call him? How did she know that he knew about Maxine Porter and Carla Garcia? What did she need to tell him about the two women?

And did he want to know? What if she wanted to tell him she knew who killed them? What if Karen Nelson confirmed his suspicions about who had murdered the women and chopped their hands off?

When he'd first seen the severed hand in Maxine Porter's condo, he'd had a feeling he knew the killer. The gruesome dismemberment was a grim memento he was too familiar with. It was like a calling card, the killer's sick, twisted signature.

The severed hand was Richard's sick, twisted signature.

Exhaling, Sione sat back in his chair. What if Karen Nelson wanted to tell him that his father had killed Maxine Porter and Carla Garcia? Did he really want to know that? Because if Richard had murdered the women, then he would have to do something.

He would have to call the cops. He would have to rat on his father.

Maybe he was getting ahead of himself, Sione decided. He didn't know what Karen Nelson wanted to tell him, so maybe he should ease up on the speculation. It was possible she knew nothing about who killed the women.

I really need to tell you what I know.

Standing, Sione headed out of his office.

21

Fifteen minutes outside of downtown San Ignacio, Sione turned the Mercedes onto a two-lane dirt road, heading toward the address Karen Nelson had given him, a house in the Bullet Tree area. An enclave for expats, it was a quiet and peaceful neighborhood where many of the homes had been renovated and were used as rental properties for tourists due to its location near the Mopan River.

The sun made its steady descent, leaving behind a hazy smear of pink and purple, as he drove past clusters of trees, a green blur of leaves and branches. Ahead, less than a quarter of a mile away, Sione spotted the house, a small ranch with a few lime trees in the front yard. Turning off the main road, the chassis rocked as he increased his speed, gravel popping and pinging beneath the car. Sione steered the sedan toward the house and then parked parallel to the porch, a long, wide veranda running along the front of the house.

He cut the engine, hesitant to get out of the car. Driving from the resort, he'd been plagued with indecision. Did he want to find out what Karen Nelson wanted to tell him about Carla Garcia and Maxine Porter? Or did he want to turn the car around, go back to the resort, and start the impossibly frustrating process of trying to pretend he had never gotten a frantic call from her?

Sione sighed. Why did the woman really want to talk to him? Was it possible Karen Nelson had some proof of Richard's crimes? Did she want him to give that proof to the police? Could he do that? Would he be able to rat his father out to the cops?

Opening the door, Sione stepped out into the heat and humidity. His shoes crunching gravel and rocks, he walked to the front door. Pushing past the reluctance, and the urge to turn and flee, Sione knocked on the door and waited. As the seconds passed, he tried to prepare himself for what he suspected Karen Nelson would tell him, but it was damn near impossible. He wasn't sure what he would do if she told him Richard had killed Carla Garcia and Maxine Porter.

Not if … *when* she told him.

"Ms. Nelson," he called out, banging on the door. "Karen? It's Sione Tuiali'i."

Seconds turned to minutes. Frustrated, Sione glanced back at the Mercedes, eager to leave, to forget about having his suspicions confirmed. Maybe he didn't need to know beyond a shadow of a doubt that his father was still in the business of taking lives.

Cicadas and crickets provided an annoying accompaniment to his closed fist thudding against the wood. Sione glanced at the doorknob. Thoughts formed, but he didn't want to acknowledge them. Despite his wariness, Sione grabbed the doorknob and twisted it. The door separated from the frame, and with a gentle push, it opened. His heart thudded. Hesitating, Sione stood just outside the entrance, staring inside.

A basic open floor plan with little imagination. A cramped living area washed in the golden glow of fading sunlight and an L-shaped kitchen with a small table. Designed to be more practical than luxurious, it was for travelers who required few amenities and just wanted a decent place to sleep and shower.

As he stepped over the threshold, Sione felt a twinge of unease, sensing something wasn't right. Another step into the living room and he realized what it was. Quiet. It was too quiet.

Apprehensive, Sione took a few steps left, scanning the sparse furnishings in the living room—a couch, coffee table, and large recliner adjacent to the couch. Frowning, Sione stared at the coffee table again, his gaze drawn to a dark, wet splotch on the bamboo surface.

He took a seat on the couch and reached a hand toward the dark, wet spot. His fingers hovered above it for a few seconds, during which a battle raged in his mind. A struggle between involvement and ignorance. Find out what the dark wetness was or get the hell out of that house before he had a chance to determine if his suspicions were true.

Swiping a pinky across the dark, wet spot, he held the finger in front of his face, inspecting it. In the slant of coppery afternoon sunlight from the kitchen window, the wetness coating the tip of his finger showed its true color. Red. Blood.

Rising from the couch, Sione saw another dark splotch on the floor between the couch and the coffee table. On his feet, heart slamming, he stared at the tile. Quarter-sized splotches crowded around his feet in a semi-circle that soon opened and formed a line.

Sione followed the blood splatters, a gruesome trail leading out of the living area, around the corner, and into a spacious bedroom. The room was dim. Hazy sunlight bathed the bed and the figure lying on top of it.

A woman, Sione could tell, sprawled on her stomach. Sione approached the bed, his pulse racing faster with each step. Much too soon, he stared at the woman's head, face down on a pillow stained with blood, her blonde ponytail trailing down her spine.

Trying to push away the panic creeping upon him, Sione pushed the body over onto its back. His pulse jumped as his eyes trailed down her right arm, from her shoulder to the crook in her elbow to her wrist ...

The right hand was missing.

Richard Tuiali'i's bloody signature.

The woman had been shot between the eyes. At close range, he could tell. Someone had been inches from her when they'd squeezed the trigger and put a bullet in her brain. Blood had pooled beneath her head, staining the pillow and soaking the strands of her blonde hair.

A strange jolt zipped through him. Eyes narrowed, Sione focused on the woman's pale face. He knew her. He knew those freckles dotting her pallid skin.

Karen Nelson.

Sione took a deep breath, trying to focus, to determine the next steps. He needed to call the San Ignacio police and tell them what had happened.

But did he really know what had happened?

A woman had been killed. Murdered in cold blood. Other than that, what did he know? Nothing. Except Karen Nelson was a former employee of Ben Chang and a stolen passport and money had been delivered to her by Spencer.

What did he know? Too damn much. And yet, not enough. Sione still had questions.

The police would have questions too. A lot of damn questions. Questions he didn't know how to answer. Questions he didn't want to answer. The cops would want to know why he had come there. And did he know the dead woman or who had killed her?

He couldn't tell them the truth, couldn't tell them he suspected his father had put the fatal bullet between Karen's eyes. But he couldn't stay quiet about the woman's murder either. Maybe he couldn't call the cops, but he could tell D.J.

His cousin had taken care of the situations with Maxine Porter and Carla Garcia. D.J. would be able to deal with Karen Nelson. But D.J. was in New York, Sione reminded himself. The damn divorce mediation. His cousin wouldn't be able to get back to San Ignacio for a few days. Maybe until next week, D.J. hadn't been sure.

Sione cursed. What the hell now?

Couldn't call Jared. He was a detective true and through. Jared would demand answers. He wouldn't let Sione get away with vague, evasive responses. Truman maybe? Maybe. Dead bodies weren't Truman's area of expertise, but he could count on Truman to be on the same page as he was about calling the cops.

Confident he and Truman could come up with a plan, Sione turned.

A piercing jolt ripped through his body, leaving him disoriented and reeling, feeling like he'd been kicked in the gut. Time seemed to stop as a strange silence settled upon him. A silky laugh, like an enticing purr, floated toward Sione and grabbed him, shocking him senseless.

"What the—"

"Yeah, I agree," she said, smiling. "This is quite a surprise."

Blood roaring through his head, Sione stared at the woman standing in the doorway.

Exotically beautiful, her dark, thick hair hung in silky ribbons, framing a heart-shaped face complimented by eyes full of mischief and a luscious mouth. Clad in a tight black T-shirt and black jeans, she was tall and lithe, and as she walked toward him, her gait was predatory, like a jungle cat. She looked beautiful and vibrant despite the gleam of mayhem and larceny in her gaze. He had a feeling she was enjoying his confusion and apprehension.

"What the hell are you doing here?" Sione asked, trying to recover from the shock, not sure he ever would, or even could.

Her smug smile highlighted the defiant and arrogant tilt of her head as she stared at him with those dark eyes, midnight with a flash of indigo.

Laughing, she said, "Don't you mean, how the hell am I still alive?"

He didn't know what to do, or think, or how to believe what the hell he was seeing.

His ex-fiancée …

Moana.

She wasn't dead.

It didn't make sense. How was she still alive? How was she standing in front of him when she had been killed during a prison riot?

"You seem to be struggling for a response." Taking a step toward him, Moana said, "I'm sure you're shocked and dismayed. But more dismayed than surprised, I suppose."

Sione said, "I'm disappointed and angry."

"Angry?" Her frown held a hint of amusement. "It's a miracle that I'm alive and you're pissed off?"

"The fact that you're alive is not a miracle," Sione said. "It's a tragedy."

Disjointed, he didn't know if he should step back or move closer to her. She was like a magnet. He'd forgotten how easy it was to be enticed into coming too close. She'd always been like a lure, drawing him into something decadent and wicked. Something hard to deny; something impossible to resist.

"I'm not surprised you feel that way," Moana said. "I didn't expect you to be happy that I wasn't stabbed to death. When you heard about my death, I'm sure you hoped I'd suffered and wished you could dance on my grave."

"The thought did cross my mind."

"Well, wishing doesn't make things so, you should know that."

"Yeah, I do," he said. "I wished for a woman who was caring and compassionate, a woman I could trust, who was as committed to me as I was to her, which was the kind of woman you tricked me into thinking you were."

"Oh, there you go, pointing out all my faults and flaws, talking about how I didn't measure up to your standards," she said. "Well, I had hopes and wishes, too. I wished and hoped for a man to love me despite my faults and flaws."

"I wished for a woman who wouldn't cheat on me with a man who hates me and—" He stopped, warning himself to let it go. Now was not the time to resurrect old feelings and feuds he still couldn't figure out how to bury.

They'd already argued, too many times, about the destruction of their relationship. They'd yelled and blamed each other about the part they'd both played in the demise of what should have been happily ever after together forever. They'd screamed about Ben's divisive role in the dismantling of what they'd mistakenly thought was a solid union.

The shouting and fighting had never accomplished anything. It only made Sione regret his decision not to break Moana's neck.

Right now, the most important thing was … what? He wasn't sure anymore. Moments ago, the most pressing issue was figuring out what to do about Karen Nelson, how to handle her death, and his suspicions about who had killed her.

Moana had caused an urgent, immediate shift in his priorities. Maybe the call to Truman would have to wait. Maybe he needed to find out how and why his ex-fiancée was alive. What was she doing at Karen Nelson's rental house? Did she know Karen Nelson? Did she know anything about Karen Nelson's death? Had Moana killed Karen Nelson? But ... what reason could his ex-fiancée have to put a bullet between the blonde's eyes? After a deep breath, he asked, "So how the hell are you still alive?"

"Well, it's an interesting story ..."

"Oh, really?" Sione asked, but it was hard to focus, and yet he had to be on guard and alert. Moana was a real and viable threat. He had to be ready for any sudden moves that might telegraph her intentions.

"Would you like to hear it?"

"Why not?" He shrugged, trying not to appear as wary and wired as he felt. "Why aren't you dead?"

"Ask your father."

"What?"

Ask your father ... the same thing Ben had said, and in the same taunting tone, almost as though daring him.

"Richard knows why I'm still alive."

"You lying bitch," he said.

"Not surprised you don't believe me." The amusement in her dark eyes turned to acrimony. "But, trust me, the whole 'Moana gets stabbed to death in a violent prison riot' plot was Richard's bright idea."

"I don't believe you," he said. "My father would never help you get out of prison. He hates you. He blames you for coming between me and Ben."

"I never came between you and Ben," she said, giving him a sly smile. "I wish I had come between you two, but you weren't down for that."

"Richard would not help you," he said, ignoring her innuendo.

"Richard came to visit me in prison," she said. "He wanted me to steal an envelope for him."

"An envelope?"

"It belonged to Ben. Really fancy, made of lambskin with a red wax stamp on the back to seal it," she said. "I don't know how, but Richard knew that Ben had told me to hide that envelope. Ben had a house in Montego Bay, and that's where I hid it, in a safe, almost two years ago."

"What's in the envelope?' Sione asked. "Why did Ben want you to hide it? Why does my father want it?"

"No clue." Moana shrugged, a smile playing at the corner of her full mouth. "I didn't care and I never asked. Figured it would be in my best interest not to know."

Sione stared at her, not sure if he believed her or not.

"Anyway, initially, I turned Richard down," she said. "Then I changed my mind. Figured I could use your father's request to my advantage. So, I had someone retrieve the envelope."

"Who?" he asked, wondering if she would be honest.

"Peter," she said. "Your cousin."

Sione glared at her. "Why the hell would you get my cousin involved in this?"

Since he'd found out about Peter's role in the stolen envelope plot, Sione had wondered how Moana had managed to make a damn fool of him, convincing his cousin to break the law.

"Peter is a good friend," Moana said, walking to the dresser and leaning a hip against the edge of it. "He's the only person in your whole family who doesn't hate me."

"So … my cousin steals the envelope for you and then what?"

"Then I told Peter to hide it for me," Moana said. "In your casita."

"*My* casita?" Sione put some outrage in his tone, figuring a bit of incredulity was needed to keep her from being suspicious. "Why the hell did you have him hide it in *my* casita?"

"I'll get to that," she said, giving him an enigmatic smile. "And it'll make sense."

Worried, he said, "So, Peter hid the envelope and then?

"I contacted your father," she said. "I offered Richard a deal. He could have the envelope if he got me out of prison."

"And that's how you got out of jail?" Sione asked. "He set up a phony fight where you would be killed?"

"No, actually that's not what happened," Moana said, smiling. "Richard told me to go to hell."

Sione had to smile at the frustration marring her features.

He wasn't surprised by his father's response. Richard didn't make deals or allow himself to be leveraged. Richard was about intimidation, not negotiation. Entertaining an offer would make him seem weak.

"So, I told my lawyer to get in touch with Ben for me." Moana pushed off the dresser and took a step toward him. "Ben and I relayed messages through Mr. Perales. I told Ben everything. And then, I offered Ben the same deal I offered your father. Get me out of jail and I'd give him that envelope. I made a stupid mistake, though."

"What was the mistake?"

"Ben didn't take my deal, either," she said. "Instead, he told me he would circumvent me. He said he wouldn't have to help me get out of jail because he would find the envelope. He thought he knew me. Thought he knew the places I might hide it. Well, I told Ben not to bother looking for the envelope because I had hidden it in a place where he would never be allowed to enter."

"My casita."

"When Richard told me to find the envelope," she said. "I decided I could use it like a carrot and dangle it over your father. But I had to make sure there was no way Richard could find the carrot. Richard would never think to look for it there. I knew he would never be welcomed in your casita so I didn't have to worry about Richard stealing the envelope from me. Ben would never be invited to your casita either. He knew that and so he sent a Trojan horse."

"Trojan horse?"

"Ben figured out that I'd hidden his envelope in your casita," she said. "So, he sent Kelsey Thomas to look for it."

"Kelsey Thomas," he echoed, thinking of how all the dots were starting to connect. But, once all the dots were connected, what the hell would they reveal? Would it be something he could face or something he'd be forced to look away from.

"You remember her? Met her at a club then took her back to the casita and banged her. You thought she liked you but she was really only interested in finding that envelope that Peter hid in your casita."

"How do you know about Kelsey Thomas?" Sione asked. "Did Ben tell you?"

"Kelsey Thomas and I are old acquaintances," Moana said, cutting her eyes toward Karen Nelson's body again. "She came to visit me in prison."

"Really?" Sione asked, pretending he didn't know. He remembered Kelsey Thomas' name on the list D.J. had given him, all the people who'd visited Moana before she'd "died." At the time, he hadn't known why Kelsey had gone to see Moana, but he'd figured they were connected by Ben Chang somehow.

"Kelsey told me Ben was forcing her to look for the envelope," Moana said. "If she found it, Ben would make sure she stayed out of prison. She wanted advice on how to get close to you ..."

The goal was for me to get into your casita, but I couldn't break in, he was really adamant about that, no forced entry, I had to get myself invited into your casita, or I had to trick my way in, and then I had to find some way to get you out of the casita so I could

"—look for the envelope," Moana was saying. "So, I gave her some advice."

"You gave her advice?" Sione asked, skeptical, remembering what Kelsey had claimed she was looking for.

I was supposed to steal your passport.

"I told her, Sione likes to rescue women so you must appear helpless," she said, taking another step closer and another quick glance at the body on the bed. "You must resist asserting yourself lest you be perceived as capable, intelligent, and self-reliant because if you are, then he won't want you. Kelsey didn't want to do it, but then I told her how big your—"

"Something doesn't make sense," he said, cutting her off, not interested in how she'd coached Kelsey Thomas to make a damn fool of him. "If you knew Ben was forcing Kelsey Thomas to look for the envelope, why did you give her advice on getting close to me? Weren't you afraid she might accidentally find it?"

"I wasn't worried about her finding it," Moana said, lifting a shoulder. "And she didn't. Silly little bitch got caught. But, of course, you know that."

"Ben's plan to circumvent you didn't work," Sione said. "So, did he rethink your offer? He changed his mind, got you out of prison so you could give him the envelope."

"Ben didn't get me out of prison," she said. "Richard did. I told you, 'Moana dies in a prison riot' was all your father's doing."

"And I told you I don't believe that," Sione said. "My father can't stand you. He wouldn't help you."

"But he did," Moana insisted. "Months after Richard turned down my offer and told me to go to hell, he reached out to me again with another offer. He would get me out of jail—"

"If you gave him the envelope?"

"That deal was no longer on the table," she said, looking up at him, a fierce amusement in her midnight gaze. "Richard had a brand new offer. He wanted me to get rid of a few loose ends."

Sione stared at her, his heart slamming. Loose ends. He'd heard his father use those words before. Loose ends. A reference to dangerous people who knew too much and had to be … taken care of. "What loose ends?"

"One of them is lying on the bed over there."

"You killed Karen Nelson?"

"How do you know her name is Karen Nelson?" she asked. "Had the two of you met before her untimely demise?"

"Why'd you kill her?"

"I told you," she said, sounding a bit impatient. "Your father wanted me to get rid of loose ends. That's why he got me out of prison. That's why he planned it so I would die in that prison fight. A dead girl can't shoot you in the head."

"Why would my father want Karen Nelson killed?" Sione asked, thinking questions might give him time to think of some way to get an advantage over her. "How did he even know her?"

"Don't know, don't care." Shrugging, Moana said, "Whatever beef they had is none of my business, but if I had to guess, it probably had something to do with Ben."

"My father wanted Karen Nelson killed because of Ben?"

"His relationship with Ben is so damn strange and convoluted. I think Richard said Ben forced Karen Nelson and the other two to betray him."

"The other two?"

"Carla Garcia and Maxine Porter."

"You killed them?"

Glaring at him, she said, "Loose ends."

"And you cut their hands off?"

"Richard's orders." Smiling, she said, "Nice clean chop."

"Why would my father want you to use his signature?"

Moana shrugged. "I'm guessing that Ben was supposed to think that Richard had killed those dumb bitches."

Staring at her, Sione wondered, who the hell was she? Certainly not the woman he'd asked to marry him. Certainly not the girl he'd met on the beach in A'arotanga when they were seventeen and sex-starved. She wasn't even something in between the two. She seemed to be something new, something he'd never dreamed she could become. Evil.

Had he ever really known her? Had prison changed her, turned her into this cruel, heartless woman glaring at him? Or had she always been this way, so ruthless and mercenary, and he just hadn't seen it? Had she hidden who she really was from him?

And if she had, how could he throw stones.

Hadn't he spent the last decade trying to hide who he really was? Trying to fight dark urges and keep people from discovering the truth about him? Desperately doing whatever he had to so he wouldn't accidentally reveal his past?

"Well, handsome, it's been a blast seeing you again," she said. "You still make me wish I had been the right girl for you, but wishing doesn't make it so, right?"

"Wait a minute, tell me this," he said. "If my father helped you get out of jail, then why did you call me with that bullshit about him wanting you dead?"

"Richard's instructions," she said. "He was hoping you would think he killed me and then you would confront him. He was trying to trick you into coming to see him. He misses you. He wants to repair your relationship. You mean everything to him."

"I doubt that," Sione said, though he knew Moana was telling the truth.

"Anyway, I need to clean up this mess I made," she said, nodding toward the bed. "And then I have one more loose end to tie up ..."

"One more loose end?" he asked, his pulse starting to race.

She gave him a look of defiant amusement and then said, "Spencer Edwards."

Something screamed and roared through his head as he stared at her, paralyzed, unable to form coherent thoughts.

"Of course, you know her," Moana said. "The sexy, good-looking black girl you're banging. I have to tell you, handsome, I'm kind of jealous. I wouldn't mind hitting that myself."

"You stay the hell away from Spencer."

"Weren't you listening?" Moana asked, frowning at him as though he were a recalcitrant child. "I told you, I have to get rid of all the loose ends. Richard's orders. Spencer Edwards is a loose end."

"That doesn't make sense," Sione said, more to himself than to Moana. "Richard doesn't know Spencer."

Shrugging, Moana said, "You know your father doesn't like to be questioned. Don't ask, because he's not going to tell."

"Stay away from Spencer."

"You don't seem to understand how it works." Moana said. "The deal was, if Richard got me out of jail, I would tie up his loose ends. He's held up his end of the bargain. I have to hold up my end. If I don't, you know what your father will do to me. They won't even find my body."

"You need to be more worried about what I'm going to do to you."

"What you're going to do to me?" Moana asked, and there was

confusion in the laugh that followed. "Oh, now you want to be a chip off the old Glock? You don't have the guts to kill me. You never did and you never will."

She glared at him, hate in her dark gaze. Her body trembled, an almost imperceptible tremor, as though rage churning deep within her was radiating out to her extremities.

Looking at her, Sione remembered the day he'd caught her with Ben. He had wanted to kill Moana, but he hadn't. His uncle's influence had been strong then, and he couldn't convince himself to put his hands around her throat and snap her neck. Big mistake.

He should have killed her when he had the chance. If he had, three women would still be alive today. Their blood was on his hands. But, he would rectify that mistake.

Moana must have seen his intentions or discerned something in his gaze. She took a step backward, and then another, and then she turned and ran.

Anticipating her actions, Sione took off after her. Out of the bedroom. Down the hall. Around the corner. Into the living room. Moana sprinted toward the door and got there quicker than he'd thought she would.

Determined not to let the bitch get away, Sione lunged and was right upon her as she clutched the knob. Before she could open the door, he grabbed her by the back of her neck and yanked her away from the door. Howling in anger, she tried to wrestle away, kicking and writhing and whirling like some Tasmanian devil.

Sione threw her into the wall. Slamming against the sheet rock, Moana gasped and then dropped to the floor. Sione went to her and dropped to his knees in front of her. Grabbing her around the throat, he yanked her to her knees. Gasping and gurgling, Moana tried to pry his hand from her throat. Nails dug into his wrist. Ignoring the pain, he tightened his hold. She slapped and punched his face, her eyes growing wider, in shock and terror, and he imagined she realized what he was planning for her and knew he would not stop until his plan succeeded.

Moana knew she was about to die. And Sione knew he was going to kill her. Not because he wanted to …

He had to kill her.

Spencer Edwards is a loose end

But that wasn't true. Spencer was becoming everything to him, and so much more. Everything he'd hoped and prayed and wished for. She was his chance at happiness. A chance he'd never thought he would have again. And he would be damned if he let Moana steal that chance from him a second time.

As Moana raked her nails against his arm, leaving behind thin, bloody welts, Sione tightened his grip, remembering the lessons Richard had given him, crushing the trachea, cutting off the flow of oxygen.

Rising to his feet, he pulled Moana up with him. Her heels and feet slapped the tile floor until he lifted her higher, eye level with him. With no solid ground beneath her, she pumped and bicycled her legs in the air, staring at him with a dark, soulless gaze.

Seconds later, her eyelids flickered, and then her pupils rolled back. Her mouth went slack and her body went limp. Panting, scarcely able to catch his own breath, Sione yanked his hand from her neck.

Moana's body fell, crashing to the tile in a sprawling heap.

22

———

San Ignacio, Belize
Belizean Banyan Resort - Owner's Casita

Sione walked into his casita and closed the door behind him. A wall sconce in the foyer gave off dim light, just enough so he wouldn't stumble into anything. All he wanted to do was crawl into bed and pull Spencer into his arms. He was wary of closing his eyes and letting sleep claim him—wary of the nightmares he was sure he'd have to contend with, the dreams about Moana.

He was still reeling from the shock of what he'd done. Had he really killed his ex-fiancée? Was Moana really dead? Because of him? Because he had put his hands around her neck and squeezed until she stopped breathing?

Continuing down the hall to the master bedroom, his worry grew, turning to panic. He had vowed to never live the life Richard had planned for him; he wasn't going to be the person his father wanted him to be, a man devoted to menace and mayhem for profit. He had promised himself he would never become that man. Sione had denounced that life, and yet tonight, he'd embraced it.

Opening the double doors, Sione was drawn toward a glow of light, a lamp on the night table. Shaky and disoriented, he walked into the bedroom and headed to the light, staring toward the bed. Spencer was sprawled across the bed on her back, wearing a skimpy pair of purple lace panties and some kind of matching see-through camisole, giving him a nice view. He gazed at her breasts, enticed by her nipples straining against the sheer fabric, thinking strange thoughts, indulging in ideas which made no sense, like coming home to Spencer every night because they were together, because they had fallen in love.

Sione shook his head, trying to forget the crazy ideas playing with his imagination. Spencer wouldn't want to be with a cold-blooded murderer.

And that's what he was.

Turning from Spencer, he staggered toward a chair in the corner of the room and dropped down into it, leaning back, extending his legs out across the hardwood floor as Moana's lifeless body flashed in his mind. He had stared at the body for a long time, trying to control the kaleidoscope of thoughts and feelings swirling within him, but they shifted and changed too quickly. Finally, he'd left the rental house.

Outside, night had taken over. Weak light from a sconce on the porch near the front door provided scant illumination as he made his way to the Mercedes. Forcing one foot in front of the other was an effort, and he felt like he was pushing through a dark, hot blanket.

Driving back to the resort, he was jittery one moment and calm the next. It was hard to figure out what he really felt about what he'd done. As soon as he thought he knew, his emotions would shift and become vague and elusive. It was surreal. For a moment, Sione wondered if he was dreaming.

And then he thought that maybe the whole incident had been a wild figment of his imagination. Maybe he'd made it all up. Maybe it was some strange psychological response to the death of Karen Nelson, which didn't really make sense because he'd seen dead bodies before. Richard had exposed him to that particular horror, and Sione hadn't been overly traumatized.

The first time had been when he was fourteen. The body was lying on the ground. The guy looked like he was just knocked out, and if not for the bullet wound in the back of his head, and the blood congealing in the dirt, he might have been mistaken for a drunk, unconscious and sleeping off a hangover.

Sione stared at the ceiling.

He liked the idea of finding Karen's dead body on the bed and killing Moana as something that was all in his mind. As he closed his eyes, he allowed himself to think he had suffered some kind of temporary break with reality.

23

"Your mother hates me," Spencer announced as she walked into the kitchen.

John stood behind the center island, staring at a small plastic basket filled with green coconuts, a small machete, and an oversized mixing bowl. "No, she doesn't," John disputed, picking up a coconut and holding it in the palm of his hand.

Doubtful, Spencer stared at him. "Yes, she does."

John picked up the machete.

"Maggie, Keisha, and India told me she hates me," Spencer said. "They said she thinks I'm the wrong woman for you. She told your Aunt Perla that she doesn't understand why you can't meet a nice girl at church."

"Come on, they're little girls," he said, holding the coconut over the mixing bowl, staring at it, as though for wisdom or knowledge.

"They don't understand half the stuff they overhear my mom and Aunt Perla gossiping about."

"Your mother thinks I'm not good enough for you," she said. "And she's probably right."

"Don't say you're not good enough for me, okay," he warned. Using the blunt edge of the knife, he tapped against the coconut, rotating it in his hand.

"Just face it, John, your mother hates me," Spencer said, watching him tap and rotate, tap and rotate, until the coconut split in half. "Your whole family hates me."

"That is not true."

"Okay, maybe not your whole family," Spencer amended, shrugging. "Just your mom. And your cousin David."

"D.J. doesn't hate you," John said, holding the coconut over the bowl, draining the juice, and then placing the halves on the counter. "He's suspicious of you."

"Suspicious is an understatement," Spencer said. "David thinks I'm a criminal. And it's kind of your fault he feels that way about me."

"My fault?" John stared at her.

Realizing she'd have to be delicate so she didn't offend him, she said, "You told David to follow me around. You told him to investigate me. He wouldn't be suspicious of me if you hadn't put those suspicions in his head."

"Well, I wouldn't have been suspicious of you if you hadn't received that banker's box with fake passports and money hidden in Xanax boxes," he said. "Which you lied about."

Folding her arms, Spencer said, "I wouldn't have lied about the contents of that banker's box if I hadn't suspected that you had opened it, which you shouldn't have done."

John glared at her, and Spencer knew she'd crossed the line. But the arguments about John's initial suspicions of her seemed to always come up, and there was no need pretending it wasn't going to be an issue.

They would always have to contend with David's investigation of her. David's surveillance had yielded damning evidence against her—the delivery of passports and money to Carla Garcia, Karen Nelson, and Maxine Porter.

Further investigations into the three women had revealed their connections to Ben Chang, which, of course, had convinced David of Spencer's connection to Ben Chang. Naturally, John had confronted her about it, and to save her relationship with John, Spencer had been forced to lie about that connection. Although, the irony was, now she wasn't even sure if she still had a connection to Ben.

A few days had passed since she'd found the envelope.

Spencer had called and texted Ben that very day, but he hadn't responded to her. Ben had yet to respond to her, though she called and texted him every day with the same message.

I found it. Contact me.

Spencer didn't know why the hell he hadn't responded, and she didn't know where the hell he could be. She worried what would happen when Ben finally returned one of her messages, because she knew one day he would, when she least suspected it. Out of the blue, Ben would be back in her life. And then what?

After she gave him the envelope, what would she do? It was a question Rae and Shady posed to her each time she called them. Was she going back to Texas or staying in Belize with John? Spencer still didn't know.

"You just have to give D.J. some time," John said. "It's hard for him to trust you because of your connection to Ben Chang."

"But I don't really have a connection to Ben Chang," Spencer lied, desperate to keep up her ruse. "I told you, I don't even really know him. I made those deliveries because I was scared and I didn't want any problems."

"I know that, but …"

"But what?" Spencer asked. "You think it's more than that? You think there's something I'm not telling you?"

"Is there something you're not telling me?"

"What would I not be telling you?"

Shaking his head, John said, "Nothing. Doesn't matter."

Spencer wasn't so sure it didn't matter.

She always worried if maybe John hadn't believed the lies she'd been forced to tell him. She'd claimed she had never met Ben Chang and the orders he'd given her had come through some "loan manager".

"Tell me," Spencer said. "What were you going to—"

A sharp, staccato knock on the French doors that opened to the back terrace made Spencer jump.

"It's Jared," John said, looking past her.

Thankful for the interruption, Spencer hurried to the door and let the detective inside. Jared greeted her, his smile polite if not friendly, but she hadn't expected a warm welcome and she never would.

"Hey, Sione," Jared called out, walking past Spencer and into the kitchen.

Closing the door, she turned and witnessed the greeting between John and Jared. At first, there was a warm, easy familial bond, but seconds later, Jared's mood became grim.

"Wish I had better news, cousin," Jared said.

"What's going on?" John asked.

Spencer's pulse jumped, as irrational fears grabbed her. Undefined terror overshadowed her, and at once, a scripture her grandmother used to say came to mind—the guilty flee when no man pursue.

"When it rains it pours," Jared said, his tone weary.

Giving his cousin a curious glance, John asked, "What do you mean?"

"Did you two hear about the dead woman those tourists found on Ambergris Caye?" Jared asked.

Too terrified to speak, Spencer managed to nod as John said, "Yeah, I think so. What about her?"

"The woman found on Ambergris Caye had been shot between the eyes and had her right hand cut off," Jared said and continued on, "Then, a week ago, some ex-pats were cave tubing and came across a dead body. She'd been executed too, shot between the eyes with her right hand cut off. Hispanic woman we identified as Carla Garcia."

An involuntary shiver passed through Spencer as the shock of Jared's words almost made her knees buckle.

Carla Garcia was dead. She'd been killed the same way Maxine Porter had, shot between the eyes before her hand had been cut off. Most likely, the same person who'd murdered Maxine had killed Carla. But who was the killer? Had Ben killed Maxine Porter and Carla Garcia? But why would he have passports and money delivered to the women if he was planning to execute them?

"Then yesterday, we got a double murder in Bullet Tree."

"Did you say Bullet Tree?" John asked, a slight tension in his tone that Spencer found odd.

Jared nodded. "Backpackers discovered the bodies yesterday. Heinous shit. Two women. One of them had been shot between the eyes and had her right hand cut off."

Her heart slamming, Spencer took a deep breath and tried not to jump to conclusions, but she couldn't help but think about Karen Nelson. She couldn't help but wonder if the blonde tomboy was the woman who'd been executed in Bullet Tree.

"The other victim was damn near mutilated."

"Mutilated?" John asked.

Jared nodded and said, "Multiple gunshot wounds to the face. Throat slit. Stabbed several times in the chest. Overkill, that's what it's called."

"Oh my God," Spencer whispered, horrified by the grisly details.

"One of the murders was impersonal, execution-style," Jared went on. "But whoever killed the other woman must have hated her and maybe wanted to punish her."

"Have you identified her?" John asked.

"Still working on it." Jared walked to the table and stood behind the empty chair directly across from Spencer. "The other victim was Karen Nelson."

Karen Nelson, Spencer thought, troubled that her speculations about the blonde tomboy's fate had been right.

"So, we have three women who were all shot once between the eyes and then had their right hands dismembered," Jared said. "And now I have to wonder if there's some crazy, ritualistic serial killer on the loose in Belize."

"Hopefully not," John said, sounding a bit distracted. "Murder in paradise is bad for business."

"Tell me about it," Jared said. "The Tourism Minister already contacted the mayor who contacted my superiors. They want these cases wrapped up as quickly and as quietly as possible."

"You have any leads?" John asked.

"Actually, that's why I'm here. I need to ask you something, Ms. Edwards," Jared said, giving her the same look the cops in Dallas had given her when she'd been interrogated after Rae had been arrested for murder. The concerned suspicion, Shady called it. A strange brew of doubt and kindness, designed to trick you into ratting yourself out.

Her heart slamming, Spencer looked at John, who seemed just as curious and worried by Jared's request as she was, and her heart slammed harder, but she managed to say, "Okay, what is it?"

"Obviously, the investigation is just starting, but I'm trying to retrace Karen Nelson's steps," Jared said and then took a seat at the table. "I want to find out everything she did from the day she arrived in Belize to the day she was killed. I'm trying to find people she might have come in contact with. We discovered she took one of those cave exploration tours—"

"Jared, most people who come to Belize visit the caves," John said. "What does that have to do with what you need to ask Spencer?"

"We asked the tour company for a list of all the people who'd been on the same tour with Karen Nelson," Jared explained, pulling a notebook from his lightweight sports jacket. "Ms. Edwards was on that list."

Spencer felt her heart plummet as she struggled to breathe, trying not to assume that Jared had come to trap her in a lie so he could arrest her for a murder she hadn't committed.

"So what?" John asked.

"So, Ms. Edwards," Jared flipped a few pages of his notebook and pulled out a piece of paper the size of an index card. "I was wondering if you might remember seeing Karen Nelson? Since the two of you were on the same cave tour. I have a photo of her."

Placing the index card on the table, Jared flipped it over, as though it were the flop in a game of Texas No-Limit, and pushed it across the smooth surface toward her.

What Spencer had thought was an index card was actually a photo of the freckle-faced blonde who'd held a gun in her face and didn't like the name on the fake passport. Her heart thudded as she stared at the photo, remembering the girl's yellow nail polish and the cheap little butterfly ring on her finger.

"You remember seeing her?" Jared asked.

Spencer glanced at John, noting the wariness in his eyes, and then at the detective.

"No," Spencer said, meeting Jared's shrewd gaze. "I don't remember seeing her."

"Are you sure?" Jared asked.

"She said she doesn't recognize the woman," John said. "And even if she did, so what?"

"If you did recognize Karen Nelson," Jared said, focusing on her. "Then I would want to know if you had spoken to her. Or if you had seen anyone else talking to her. I'd want to know if you noticed anything strange or out of the ordinary about her."

Shaking her head, Spencer glanced at John.

"I don't remember her," Spencer said. "I'm sorry."

"That's okay." Jared put the photo of Karen Nelson back in his notebook and then stood. "Thanks, anyway. I appreciate your cooperation." Jared gave her a skeptical smile and then looked over at John. "Sione, walk me out."

24

San Ignacio, Belize
Belizean Banyan Resort - Owner's Casita

Outside on the terrace, Jared turned to Sione. "You think Ms. Edwards is telling me the truth?"

"Why wouldn't she tell you the truth?" Sione asked, taking a few steps away from his cousin, toward the wall of hibiscus trees. "What would she have to hide?"

"Plenty," Jared said. "According to D.J."

"What the hell did D.J. tell you?"

"Just that he was worried about you getting mixed up with a woman he didn't think you should trust."

"Did he tell you why he thinks I shouldn't trust Spencer?"

"He didn't get into all that."

"You can't listen to D.J.," Sione said, relieved that D.J. had kept his mouth shut about Spencer's Xanax deliveries. "He doesn't like her."

"I hope she's telling the truth, for your sake."

"For my sake?"

"You don't need to be involved with another lying bitch like—"

"Let's not talk about *her*, okay, please," Sione said, trying to ignore any thoughts of how he'd wrapped his hands around Moana's neck, trying to forget that he'd killed her.

Even though he wasn't sure he had …

Sione had thought Moana was dead when she'd slumped to the floor, limp and unmoving. But he hadn't made sure. He'd only assumed. And for his assumption, he'd gone through hell, reliving the moment over and over, torn between anguish and apathy, and self-condemnation and self-justification. All the mental turmoil might have been for nothing.

Double murder … one of them shot between the eyes … the other one damn near mutilated

The other one.

Sione knew it was Moana. What he didn't know was how she'd died. And who had killed her? Maybe it wasn't him. He'd choked her, but maybe not to death. What he'd assumed was her lifeless body might have been her unconscious form. After Sione had left, someone had shot Moana and stabbed her, mutilating her in the process of taking her life.

Who the hell had done that?

Whoever killed the other woman must have hated her.

Sione couldn't pretend he didn't hate Moana. But he hadn't shot her, stabbed her, and slit her throat. It was possible that he hadn't killed her. He didn't know if he should feel relieved because it meant he wasn't like his father or if he should feel inadequate because it meant Moana was right about him. *You don't have the guts to kill me.*

"I need to tell you something about Moana," Jared said reluctantly.

"I'm sure it's not something I'm interested in hearing."

"You need to hear it," Jared said, his gaze sober, almost apologetic. "Even though I'm not really sure how to say it."

"Jared, I don't—"

"Moana is dead."

"I know." Sione stared at him.

"You know?" Jared echoed, shock registering on his face.

"Her lawyer called me shortly after it happened," Sione said. "He told me she was killed in a prison fight."

Sione took a breath, wanting to blurt out the truth. Moana didn't die in some prison fight. He knew that for a fact. Three days ago, he'd seen her. She had stood in front of him, giving him that haughty stare with those indigo eyes, telling him some crazy story about faking her death.

Richard's idea, she claimed, but Sione wasn't sure if his father had orchestrated the gruesome events.

Ask you father.

But he couldn't. He wouldn't. He didn't want to know.

Jared said, "I'm sorry."

Sione stared at his cousin. "Why the hell are you sorry?"

"Well … " Jared paused for a moment and then said, "You were once in love with Moana and you were going to marry her and—"

"My relationship with her was so damn long ago, I hardly remember—"

"It was two years ago," Jared reminded him. "Not that long. And despite what happened between you two, and how things ended, I know the last thing you wanted was for her to end up dead."

Sione didn't say anything. How could he respond when he felt like he'd just been kicked in the balls. But he had to say something because Jared's sympathetic gaze was starting to look more like confusion, and soon the confusion would turn to suspicion.

"No, you're right." Sione forced the words from his mouth. "That's the last thing I ever wanted."

25

San Ignacio, Belize

Belizean Banyan Resort - Owner's Casita

As soon as John walked back into the kitchen, Spencer said, "Your cousin thinks I'm lying, doesn't he?"

"Lying about what?"

"About knowing Karen Nelson."

"He asked me if you were telling the truth."

"And what did you say?"

"What do you think I said?"

"John, please—"

"Don't you trust me by now? Don't you know I'm on your side?" he asked. "Why do you think I would I ever rat you out? I'm not going to get you in trouble and have you arrested and taken from me. I told you, I'm going to protect you."

"I do trust you, John," she said. "I don't mean to make you think that I doubt you, I just … I wish you didn't have to keep all my secrets."

"I can deal with the secrets and the lies," he said. "Because if not for the secrets and lies, I guess you wouldn't be here. As hard and dangerous as this situation with the favor has been for you, I have to be grateful, because if you had been able to pay back that loan, then you wouldn't have been sent to Belize to make those deliveries and I wouldn't have met you."

"You don't have to say that, John."

"Yeah, I do." John walked to the table, took her hand, and pulled her up. "Because it's the truth, and I want you to know how I feel about you."

The way he looked at her was a bit different as he put his arms around her, pulling her closer to him. Looking up at him, Spencer wondered if John loved her. The thought was dizzying, leaving her both ecstatic and terrified. Her heart pounded and she felt a fluttering panic in her chest. What would she do if John told her that he loved her? Would she tell him that she loved him, too? But was that true? Did she love John?

Seconds later, he kissed her, a long, slow kiss that she never wanted to end. He hadn't told her he was in love with her, and she was a bit disappointed, but a larger part of her was relieved. She didn't think either of them was ready for the L-word. Because once it was said, it would be out there between them. They wouldn't be able to take it back if one of them changed their minds.

"Anyway," he said, pulling away gradually. "You don't know anything about Karen Nelson. You were told to deliver a box of Xanax to her—"

"Which had a fake passport and money in it."

"You weren't told anything about the contents," John reminded her. "You were just told to deliver them."

"I know," Spencer said. "But I made those deliveries to Karen Nelson, Carla Garcia, and Maxine Porter, and now they're all dead. And I just feel like …"

"Like what?"

"Like I should tell the police that they got money and fake passports from that guy Ben Chang."

"I don't think that's a good idea," John said. "First of all, you don't have any proof. You never met Ben Chang. He didn't tell you himself to make those deliveries."

Her heart lurched, and Spencer looked down, afraid John would see her deception reflected in her eyes.

"And even if he had," John went on. "He would just deny it. Probably say he doesn't know you or what you're talking about."

"I know, but," Spencer sighed and ventured to look at him again. "Three women are dead because—"

"I know you're upset about what happened to those women," John said. "But I know it wasn't your fault, and I don't think you could have prevented it. And I don't think you can help the cops with this investigation. Those women were involved with dangerous people, and they were living dangerous lives, and that's why they were killed."

Too distraught to speak, Spencer stepped closer to John as he embraced her.

"We already decided that we're going to put all that business with you making those deliveries behind us, remember?" he said. "You were forced to do it, you did it, and it's over. So, now let's concentrate on me and you, okay?"

Spencer nodded her agreement as she closed her eyes and rested her head on his chest, knowing that her business with Ben Chang was far from over. It wouldn't be completely finished until Ben had the envelope and she had the video he'd used to blackmail her.

26

San Ignacio, Belize
Shawville Subdivision

Taking deep, measured breaths, Spencer tried to relax as the shuttle sped away from the resort. As she glanced over her shoulder out the back window, the resort seemed a lifetime away as the shuttle took her toward the center of town.

Like Lot's wife, looking back at the life she yearned for, Spencer felt if she stared too long she would turn into a pillar of salt, destroyed by some desire for a chance she didn't deserve with a man she had a feeling she would never be good enough for.

Thinking of John, she cringed, wishing she hadn't had to lie to him.

Before leaving, Spencer had sent John an email saying she was going to a neighboring hotel to check out a local art exhibit they were hosting, an event she'd seen in the small neighborhood circular she had found in the resort lobby.

But he couldn't know the truth.

Earlier that morning, after John had left for the office, one of the bellmen had delivered her a note. Inside, the message had sent a jolt of panic, disappointment, and fear through her. Ben wanted to see her today. There was an address where the meeting would take place. The last line warned *don't be late sweet girl …*

Sighing, Spencer checked her watch. 5:21 p.m. She was supposed to meet Ben at 5:30 p.m. at a house in some neighborhood she knew nothing about. The driver had nodded when she'd told him her destination and assured her he would get her there on time.

Not that she was anxious to arrive at the designated meeting place. She was nervous about seeing Ben again, face to face; it had been a few weeks since that morning in his kitchen when he'd forced her into the unenviable position of having to do him a "favor" to secure her freedom.

The shuttle turned up a small hill on a quiet street. Her pulse jumped. It wouldn't be long now. Soon, she'd be out of the shuttle, knocking on the door, and then face to face with Ben. And what would happen when she saw him again?

Ben hadn't mentioned the envelope in his note, but he didn't have to. Spencer knew they were meeting to make the exchange they'd previously agreed to—the envelope for her passport, the plane ticket back to Houston, and the video of her stealing from him.

Spencer thought about the envelope, resting at the bottom of her Birkin. Why did Ben want the envelope? What was sealed inside the lambskin? Rae thought she should have opened it, but Shady had said it would have been like opening Pandora's box.

Spencer had agreed. The contents of the envelope didn't matter. All she wanted was to give Ben the envelope and get her passport.

Once her passport was in her hand, then what? Would she leave Belize? Get on a plane and go back to Houston? Back to some temporary assignment she hoped might become a permanent position with vacation and benefits?

If she stayed in Belize, then what? Would she actually have a chance to be with John? A chance to see if "something" really was happening between them?

Her feelings for John were deepening and lengthening day by day. And yet, her old doubts and issues lingered. Spencer wasn't sure she wanted love and romance and a soul mate.

The shuttle slowed and then stopped in front of a modest two-story house surrounded by trees and flowering bushes. The small yard was enclosed by a chain-link fence, and security bars covered the windows.

After thanking the driver, she exited the shuttle, her heart slamming. It was a balmy night, breezy with a whiff of rain in the wind. On shaky legs, she walked through the gate and up the gravel drive toward the front door, passing large, leafy banana trees lined along the fence.

At the door, Spencer hesitated and thought of turning around and running for her life down the dark street. But no longer willing to prolong the inevitable, Spencer knocked on the door. Minutes later, when it opened, she froze.

The man standing at the door was not Ben Chang.

27

Before Spencer could scream her protest, Tommy Fong reached out and grabbed her arm.

"Let go of me!" Spencer stiffened, heart thudding as she tried to resist, but his hold was like a shackle as he yanked the Birkin from her, threw it to the floor, and pulled her into the house.

Behind her, the door slammed. Terror gripped her, making its way around her throat, threatening to strangle the life from her.

"You not going to get away this time, bitch," he said, manhandling her toward a lumpy, brown sectional couch in the middle of the living area.

"What are you—"

Fong gave Spencer a backhanded slap that set her face on fire and sent her stumbling to the floor. Sprawled on the cool tile, Spencer struggled up on all fours as Fong came at her, a deep vertical crease in the middle of his forehead. Reaching down, he grabbed her hair, pulling the strands from her chignon. Screaming, Spencer kicked him in the ankle and then rolled over, across the floor, losing her right shoe as she scrambled to her hands and knees again. Crawling to the couch, she pulled herself up and glanced over her shoulder.

Fong was behind her. Shaking, panic and adrenaline swirling in her veins, Spencer stumbled around the couch and toward the kitchen, her gaze trained on a door next to the refrigerator. A hand clamped around her ankle. Spencer cried out and crashed to the floor, banging her elbow and her hip. Ignoring the pain, palms on the floor, she fought to pull herself forward as Fong tried to yank her back.

"No!" She kicked her leg back and felt her heel connect with flesh. Fong grunted, his fingers loosening around her ankle, and she kicked again, this time feeling something wet and slippery as her toes made a connection.

Howling, Fong dropped her foot. Spencer dragged herself to her feet. Stumbling and hobbling to the door, she looked over her shoulder. Staggering to his feet, Fong lurched toward her. Flinging the door open, Spencer stumbled out of the house.

Wild and desperate, she ran haphazardly, heading into a tangle of trees. Stumbling, she kicked off her remaining shoe and then continued barefoot through the trees. Confused and disoriented, she pushed past the leaves, vines, and branches surrounding her, enveloping her in a cool shroud, blocking the late afternoon sun.

She needed to get to the road. If she could get to the road, she could find her way back to the resort, someway, somehow. As she sprinted through the hanging vines and past the thick leaves, she realized something was wrong. She was running in the wrong direction.

She'd escaped through the door next to the refrigerator, but she hadn't entered the house through that door. Desperate and panicked, in her haste to get away from Fong, she'd made the mistake of running out of the back door.

With sickening terror, Spencer skidded to a stop and turned around.

Fong was racing toward her.

28

———————

San Ignacio, Belize
Belizean Banyan Resort - Owner's Casita

It was 6:34 p.m. Sione stood in his bedroom, staring at the space where Spencer slept wrapped in his arms every night. When he woke up every morning, he couldn't help but think how perfect she felt next to him, as if she were meant to be there. He wondered if she felt the same way about him as he felt about her.

Though he couldn't say for sure how he felt about Spencer.

He didn't think he was in love with her. He couldn't be. Not yet, anyway. They hadn't known each other long enough for him to be in love with her, he didn't think. But maybe he was heading in that direction.

The question was, did he want to? Spencer was beautiful and exciting, sometimes even goofy and funny. But she could be selfish and abrasive, too. He wasn't sure he wanted to fall in love with a woman who was fierce and a bit demanding, no matter how sexy she was.

Sione stared at the bed, unable to shake the apprehension he felt. He hadn't seen Spencer since early this morning, and all he'd wanted to do when he got back to the casita was pull her into his arms, and into the bedroom, but she wasn't there. Earlier, she'd sent him an email about an art show at a neighboring resort she'd gone to. Sione had found a listing for the event in the circular newspaper, and the show was from 4:00 to 6:00 p.m.

The event was over, but Spencer wasn't back yet. He didn't want to start worrying, but he couldn't stop thinking about Moana's promise.

Spencer is next.

Sione exhaled and forced himself to think rationally, logically. He couldn't let Moana's threats haunt him. Moana was dead. He wasn't sure if it was by his hands or someone else's. Either way, he knew she was dead.

Spencer is next.

No, that wasn't true. Moana couldn't hurt Spencer. He shouldn't even be thinking of Spencer being hurt or in some sort of trouble. Those were baseless conclusions he had no reason to jump to, but still he was worried. Sione couldn't shake the foreboding feelings, sly as serpents, coiled within him. Try as he might, he couldn't stop himself from thinking something bad was going to happen.

29

San Ignacio, Belize
Outskirts of Cahal Pech

Spencer's bare feet pounded the jungle floor as the trail snaked to the right and then abruptly curved left. She flew between two sandalwood trees and jumped over roots slithering across the forest bed. Increasing her speed, she glanced back again. Fong was too close behind her, steadily cutting the distance between them.

Panting, she skidded on leaves as the trail twisted and snaked, forcing her down a steep slope, one she had to slow down to navigate or risk falling on her ass. She felt her stamina fading, and forcing her burning legs to keep going was almost insurmountable. Spencer glanced back again, looking for Fong. She didn't see him.

Adrenaline surged through Spencer, strong and heady. She lurched forward, afraid to stop and catch her breath. Fong might be trying to trick her, trying to fool her into thinking he'd given up the chase. Too scared to look back again, afraid she might see Fong behind her, she forced herself to run faster.

A thousand thoughts swirled in her mind, questions and worries. One thought prevailed, demanding her attention. *Would she ever see John again?* Gulping air, Spencer kept going, propelled by fear and desperation as the question haunted her. *Would she get the chance to tell him how she felt about him? Would she—*

An arm snaked around her neck, tightening around her throat. Terrified, Spencer tried to scream, but when she opened her mouth, a strangled gurgle escaped. Clamping her hands down onto Fong's arm, Spencer clawed at his skin, trying to pull his arm away. Gasping and panting, she bucked and jerked, trying to escape, but the more she fought, the more exhausted she became until a strange, deep cloud descended upon her and everything went black.

30

Sione paced from one end of the living room to the other and back again. Spencer hadn't returned from the art show, and he was trying not to get anxious. Shouldn't she be back by now? How long did it take to look at a bunch of paintings she wasn't going to buy anyway?

Clutching his cellphone, Sione sat down on the couch and then stood up. Then he sat again and sent Spencer another text, the fifth, or maybe sixth, message, asking her where she was and telling her to call him immediately and let him know she was okay. So far, each text had gone unanswered, and she hadn't called.

He tried not to worry and told himself not to jump to any unfounded conclusions, like Spencer hadn't called him because she couldn't, because she wasn't okay. There was no need to think the worst. After all, Spencer was tough, right? Wasn't she always telling him she could take care of herself? Her fierce independence and her bad girl posturing was one of the things about her he found both alluring and infuriating.

Standing, Sione pushed the thought away, unwilling to let his mind go there, and walked into the kitchen, trying to stay calm, and glanced at the wall clock. 8:02 p.m. Maybe he should call the police?

What would he tell them? Spencer was an adult. If she wanted to leave the resort, she had every right to do so. And she probably wouldn't want him calling the cops or leading some search party to look for her. Hadn't she told him she didn't need to be rescued?

Yeah, but he wasn't sure if that was true, wasn't sure he believed all her protests against the knight in shining armor.

I don't need a hero.

Well, too damn bad. Spencer didn't want a hero, but he wasn't going to let her get hurt.

Hesitant, Sione went to the table and sat. Maybe he was jumping to conclusions too quickly. Maybe Spencer was fine. Maybe she really had gone to look at art. But Sione couldn't assume anything. He had to make sure Spencer was okay.

Resolved with his decision, Sione dialed the front desk. When the employee on duty answered, he asked, "What shift are you working?"

"Noon to nine p.m., Mr. Tuiali'i."

Sione cleared his throat and then asked, "Did you happen to see Ms. Edwards leave the hotel this afternoon? Maybe around three?"

"Yes, sir, I called her a cab," the employee said. "But she said it was taking too long, so Raul offered to give her a ride in the shuttle."

31

Turning off the main road, Raul steered the shuttle between an opened chain-linked gate and into the grass-and-gravel driveway.

In the front seat, next to Raul, Sione leaned forward, trying to see. "This is where you dropped her off?"

Darkness shrouded the area. The lone source of light, a street lamp yards away, offered feeble illumination, barely enough to make out the bushes lining the perimeter of the fence.

The house was modest, two-stories and surrounded by a low chain-linked fence with a yard full of banana trees. Why had Spencer told Raul to bring her to this house? Why had she lied to him about going to the art show? What was she keeping from him? Why was she still keeping things from him? Why wouldn't she tell him what was going on?

He couldn't help but think that Spencer's trip to this house had something to do with her reasons for coming to Belize.

Fake passports and money. The favor she'd been forced to do to satisfy a debt she would never have been able to pay. A chance to get out of her predicament, given to her by some asshole who did dirty work for Ben Chang. The offer seemed to be for her benefit. Or so she'd been tricked into believing. Acceptance had been to her detriment. Her debt would never be satisfied. Ben would always want her to do one more thing ... or else.

Sione suspected she'd been forced to do another Xanax box delivery. Spencer had been summoned to this house because of Ben Chang. Sione wanted to kill the son of a bitch. He wanted to put his hands around Ben's neck and squeeze until the bastard's lungs exploded and he choked to death.

"She didn't say anything about who she was going to visit?"

"She didn't really say anything," Raul said, shifting the shuttle to park. "Just thanked me for the ride."

"And you don't have any idea who lives here?"

Raul shook his head and then said, "I think it's one of those vacation properties."

"I'm going to see if she's still inside the house." Sione opened the door and jumped out of the shuttle. Crossing the yard, he walked toward the house, his apprehension mounting as he approached the front door.

With a deep breath, Sione grabbed the knob and twisted. Pushing the door open, he crossed the threshold. His eyes swept the room, taking in the lumpy sectional and behind that, a dining table and past that, the galley kitchen. At first glance, nothing seemed disturbed or out of order.

He ventured farther in, passing a reclining chair and a large entertainment shelf. Nothing was broken. There was no glass on the floor and no upended furniture. He saw no signs of struggle or strife. No evidence that anything horrible had happened, or—

He stopped, his eyes drawn to something on the floor behind the couch.

Spencer's purse.

Apprehensive, he walked to the purse, then reached down, and picked it up. Staring at the expensive bright blue bag, he knew Spencer wouldn't have dropped it. There was no way she would have left behind a twenty-thousand-dollar purse—unless there was some reason why she hadn't been able to hold on to it.

Had she been running from someone? Maybe the Asian man with the green snake tattoo? But that didn't make sense. Spencer would never have come to this house if she knew that son of a bitch was here waiting for her.

He didn't want to think the worse, but it was hard not to imagine that something bad had happened to her.

Pushing away the worrisome thoughts, Sione turned, his gaze sweeping the kitchen and—

What was that?

Sione walked to the kitchen table, his heart racing as he struggled to contend with two separate, but equally disturbing, discoveries.

The kitchen door was slightly open.

And a woman's pink canvas deck shoe lay abandoned, on its side, next to one of the table legs.

He stared at the shoe, knowing it was Spencer's. Why the hell was it lying on the floor? Sione glanced at the back door again. Why was it open? Had Spencer run out of that door, desperate to escape someone? Or had she been chased outside?

Crossing the kitchen to the door, he flung it all the way open and stepped out into the dark, humid night, calling out to Spencer. Over and over, he yelled her name, his voice growing louder until it was a hoarse, demanding plea, begging a response.

But there was none.

32

San Ignacio, Belize
Shawville Subdivision

Sione opened the shuttle door. "You have a flashlight in here?"

Raul nodded and asked, "Ms. Edwards wasn't in there?"

"No, she wasn't, but I think ..." Sione trailed off, remembering the purse and the shoe, trying to control the wave of fear washing over him, threatening to pull him under.

"Mr. Tuiali'i?" Raul stared at him, wide-eyed, waiting.

"Listen," Sione took a breath, forcing himself to keep it together and concentrate. "I'm going to look behind the house. You drive around the block a few times and see if you see her walking down one of the side roads."

As the shuttle sped off, Sione headed back to the house, gripping the flashlight. With each step, his rage mounted, and by the time he'd burst through the front door, the anger had damn near consumed him.

Heading out the back door, Sione splashed the flashlight from left to right, revealing a thin strip of neglected grass that gave way to sparse jungle.

Worried, but determined, he headed through a slight gap in the bushes. Twigs and limbs cracked and snapped beneath his feet as he moved over the leaves and grass, the shaft of bluish light leading the way down the path stretching before him.

It was a balmy night, the humidity smothering, suffocating, the breeze lost in the trees. Heart pounding, Sione shined the light down the path, a thin ribbon of dirt through thick trees.

He didn't like the idea of Spencer running for her life through the forest. He didn't like the idea of her running barefoot from whoever the hell had lured her to the small, dilapidated house. Cursing, Sione whipped the flashlight back and forth, peering through the leaves, desperate to find something, *anything,* to give him a lead or some hope that he would find her.

Skirting around a group of trees, Sione bandied the flashlight like a sword, ignoring the bugs and gnats buzzing around his face. Spencer wouldn't have had to run if she had told him what the hell was going on.

Why didn't she trust him? When she'd told him about the favor and her indirect connection to Ben Chang, he'd been understanding and supportive. He hadn't judged her choices; he hadn't condemned her actions. Didn't she know he was on her side? Didn't she realize he wouldn't let anything bad happen to her? Why wasn't she convinced? Did she still think he was trying to be a hero? Did she still believe he only wanted to help her so he could feel better about himself?

He'd thought she'd given up resisting and refusing his efforts to be there for her. If Spencer wasn't so determined to be independent, she wouldn't have had to come to this house, scared and alone, thinking she had to face the consequences of her mistakes by herself.

Sione jogged along the path, slapping away broad leaves, jungle vines, and outstretched branches scratching at his skin.

He wanted to kill whoever had chased Spencer out into the dark jungle.

He waited for the murderous thought to shame him, to condemn him for reverting to the sins of his father. The self-recrimination he expected didn't come. Maybe right now, with Spencer's life at stake, he needed to be more like Richard. Ruthless. Deadly. With no apology for what he might have to do to anyone who thought they could hurt Spencer and get away with it.

Moments later, the light caught a flash of something to the right of him through the banana trees ahead. Crashing through bushes, he made his way to the tree and then focused the beam of light on the sliver of pink near the base of the trunk.

Sione stopped in his tracks, his heart thudding as he reached down and picked up the object.

Spencer's other pink deck shoe.

Galvanized by fears of Spencer alone in the jungle and barefoot, Sione splashed the light from left to right, illuminating trees, branches, and vines.

Shouting her name, Sione pushed through the dense foliage. He promised himself he would find her. If it meant searching every inch of the Belizean jungle, he would do it. He wouldn't rest until she was curled up in his arms again.

33

San Ignacio, Belize
Location Unknown

Something cold and wet hit Spencer's face, sloppily slapping across her skin, invading her nostrils, and slipping into her slightly parted lips. Gasping, Spencer swallowed and then coughed as her eyes opened and she sat forward.

Eyes flickering, she glanced up and then to the right, her head lolling as she struggled to raise it, struggled to figure out what the hell was wrong with her. Why couldn't she lift her head? Was she drunk? Her chin dropped to her left shoulder, and she opened her eyes wide, forcing herself to concentrate.

She tried to think but couldn't remember how. There was nothing in her mind but confusion. Desperate, she tried to remember ... something, *anything*. Her thoughts yielded nothing. Everything was a blank.

Spencer forced herself to look around. As her gaze adjusted to the dim lighting, the apprehension increased until she trembled, terrified and dazed. The room around her was small and warm. The air teemed with tropical humidity so thick it was almost tangible. She could feel it hovering over the layer of sweat coating her skin.

Sparkling dust particles twirled in the rays floating through the window. It wasn't large but seemed wide enough to crawl through. Instead of curtains, it was draped with spider webs, dotted with small insects and flies encased in gray cocoons to be enjoyed later by the arachnid. Flying insects buzzed and popped as they took off from one wall and landed across the room on the other.

Beside the mattress, inside the small, hot room was a ten-speed bicycle missing a tire, several cans of paint, and an old-fashioned school desk, its spindly, corroded legs struggling to hold it up.

She glanced down to her right. The floor was dirt, hard-packed earth, but she wasn't sitting on the floor. Beneath her, she felt a springy lumpiness and realized she was on a thin mattress. The padded cover was torn and snagged, stained with dark splotches and splatters, reeking of urine, which might have been her own, judging from the dampness she felt between her legs.

Where the hell was she? And how had she gotten here? How long had she been there? How long had she been knocked out?

Trying not to choke, Spencer coughed again and tried to breathe as water slid down her forehead, traveling over her cheeks and dripping from her chin onto her wrists. Water trailed into her eye, and she blinked rapidly as her eye began to sting. Vaguely, she was aware that she wanted to rub her eye.

She started to move her left hand and winced, giving a short, startled cry as pain shot across her left wrist and then surrounded it. What was wrong? Why was there pain in her wrist? Had she broken it? Worried, Spencer glanced down at her left hand.

Panic joined the confusion. Her left wrist was crossed over her right wrist. Both were tied together, bound too many times to count with thin, braided rope, the straw-like fibers smudged with dirt and possibly grease.

Staring at her hands, she felt her stomach pitch, and she swallowed hard, praying she wouldn't get sick from the horror and confusion swirling in her mind, making her dizzy and nauseous.

Her hands were tied.

Something scratched her right ankle. Wary, her gaze traveled from the tips of her fingers to her lap, where the fabric of her dress was torn and stained, and then to her bare knees, scraped and scratched, and finally to her ankles. Rope surrounded them.

Tears threatened, but she pressed her lips together. She couldn't cry. Now was not the time for tears. She had to figure out what had happened to her. She had to find out why she was tied up. Who had bound her hands and feet? Why—

The memories came back, abrupt and brutal, like bullets slamming into her brain. She'd been tricked.

Come see me, sweet girl.

She'd followed the instructions on the note. She'd been anxious to see Ben, anxious to give him the envelope. His note sent a surge of relief flowing through her. All she wanted to do was give him the envelope so she could get the video he'd used to blackmail her.

It would be a simple exchange. Then she could go on with her life. Without the evidence of her mistakes hanging over her head, she was free to start her life over. Without the fear of going to prison, she could revisit herself. She was hoping to be the person she'd been before all the mistakes. She wanted to be the woman she'd once been before all the bad decisions.

After getting out of the shuttle, she'd hurried across the gravel driveway to the house. Ben hadn't been at the door. An image of the green snake tattoo appeared before her, vivid, standing in relief against tight, sallow skin, and she had the feeling if she stared at it long enough, the green snake would move. Slithering, it would hiss at her, coiling its body and—

Hands clapped, loud and harsh. "You wake, bitch?"

Jostled, her heart slamming, Spencer's eyes widened. Crouched at the end of the mattress, sitting on his heels, Tommy Fong glared at her.

Spencer screamed.

34

"You wanted to see me." D.J. walked into Sione's office and then frowned at him. "What the hell happened to you?"

Sione exhaled, not surprised by his cousin's reaction to his appearance.

He looked like he'd been running through the jungle all night. There were scratches on his face and arms. He hadn't showered and he was still wearing the same clothes he had on yesterday, the t-shirt and jeans now stained and torn.

"I was out all night because—"

"Out all night?" D.J. gaped. "Where? In the middle of the damn jungle?"

Sighing, Sione said, "Actually, yeah."

D.J. looked confused. "What?"

"I don't have a lot of time to explain," Sione said. "Spencer is missing. I need to find her, and I need you to help—"

"Wait, what?" D.J. interrupted. "Did you just say Spencer is missing?"

Sione glared at D.J. "Did I stutter? Do you no longer understand English? Spencer is missing, and I need to find her. So I need the information you found on the guy who was eating breakfast with Spencer a few weeks ago. You said he gave her a gift. What was his name?"

"Why do you think Spencer is missing?" D.J. asked, crossing his arms.

"Yesterday, she told me she was going to an art show," Sione said. "But that wasn't true."

"So, she lied to you. Shocking."

Sione took a breath, trying to control his emotions. "I'm not jumping to conclusions. Yesterday, Spencer had one of the shuttle drivers drop her off at a house in Shawville. I went to look for her at that house. She wasn't there, but I found her purse and one of her shoes. The back door was open, and I went outside. I found the other shoe in the jungle behind the house. Somebody had chased her out of the house and into the jungle. I looked for her all night, and I couldn't find her. Whoever chased her must have taken her. And that is how I know she's missing."

"Maybe that's not the only explanation," D.J. said, his skeptical glance just shy of outright disbelief.

"What other explanation could there be?" Sione said, angry and defensive.

"Maybe she left on her own."

"She wouldn't do that," Sione said.

"Maybe she left because her job here in Belize is done," D.J. said.

"She made her Xanax deliveries—which turned out to be for nothing since all three women she delivered to are dead now."

"She didn't have anything to do with the deaths of those women," Sione said.

"But she knows something," D.J. insisted.

"Maybe she does," Sione conceded. "But I can't focus on that right now. I need to find her. Somebody chased her through the jungle and they caught her. Somebody took her, and I don't expect you to understand why I want to find her, because you think she's a lying bitch who's getting what she deserves because—"

"Wait, stop. Listen to me," D.J. said. "Don't tell me I don't understand, okay? I know how you feel about her. I don't like it, but I understand it. You care about her, I get that."

Sione pressed a thumb against the center of his forehead, trying to rub out the numbing ache that was starting to throb beneath his skull, an ache spurred by the fear and anger growing inside him.

"You got any ideas about who took her?"

"Ben Chang," Sione said.

Taking a seat, D.J. said, "You think Chang took her?"

"He had somebody do it," Sione said. "Maybe the Asian man with the green snake tattoo or the guy she had coffee with."

"William Bermudez."

"I have no leads on the Asian guy, but you said you found out where Bermudez was staying," Sione said. "I need his address. I need to talk to him."

"You think Ben told Bermudez to kidnap Spencer?"

"I think he knows about the kidnapping," Sione said. "And that son of a bitch is going to tell me what he knows."

35

____

San Ignacio, Belize
Bullet Tree Village

Sione jerked the wheel of the Mercedes to the left, turning the German sedan into the driveway of William Bermudez's rental house.

Riding shotgun, D.J. grabbed the dashboard, cursing as Sione gunned the engine and sped up the narrow strip of gravel toward the front entrance. Ignoring his cousin's demands to slow down, Sione braked hard, shifted gears, and then cut the engine. Before D.J. could get his seatbelt off, Sione was out of the car and running to the front door.

Wrapping his hands around the iron bars barring the door, Sione yanked and pulled, knowing it was no use. He wasn't getting into the house through the front door or the front windows either. They were barred too.

"Don't think he's around," D.J. said, stopping next to him. "Come on, let's go."

"Go where?" Sione glared at D.J., pissed that his cousin had refused to give him Bermudez's address unless Sione agreed to let him tag along.

"Bermudez is not here," D.J. said.

"Just because he didn't answer the door doesn't mean he's not home," Sione said and, despite D.J.'s protests, he ran around the side of the house, heading down the length of the one-story dwelling toward the backyard. He jumped the chain-link gate and walked across ankle-high grass to a back door. No security bars.

Stepping back from the door a few feet, he raised his leg and kicked the door. Then he turned sideways and rammed his shoulder into the door. He kicked again. The door groaned and flew backward into the house, banging against a wall. Barreling into the house, Sione yelled out to Bermudez. Then he called Spencer's name, praying she would answer.

He heard nothing except his own frustrated curses as he stalked from room to room, searching, hoping to find Bermudez cowering in a corner or maybe knocked out cold because Spencer had hit him over the head and found her way out. There was no sign of Bermudez. No sign of Spencer.

"You can't stay here," D.J. said, stalking into the kitchen. "You don't know if Bermudez is coming back. You don't know if he's still staying at this place."

"There are dirty dishes in the sink," Sione said, pointing at a plate littered with crumbs. "And there's food in the refrigerator. He's coming back, and I'm going to be waiting for him."

D.J. shook his head. "I don't think that's a good idea."

"I don't care what you think," Sione said. "I am not leaving, but you can go. I don't need you to stay here and keep me company. Didn't even want you to come in the first place."

"So now you don't need my help anymore?"

"I know you don't want to be here," Sione said. "You think I'm wasting my time looking for her. You think she snuck away in the middle of the night because whatever scam she pulled is over and she's moving on to the next dumb asshole stupid enough to believe her lies."

Exhaling, D.J. said nothing, but he didn't have to. His disapproving scowl said it all, loud and clear.

"Spencer didn't leave because she wanted to," Sione said. "Somebody took her, and I know Ben is the reason she's gone. He probably told Bermudez to grab her."

"Grab her for what?" D.J. asked, frowning. "You keep saying Ben took her. Why would he do that?"

"Because that's what Ben does to women," Sione said. "He uses them and then he discards them."

"So, Ben told Spencer to make the Xanax box deliveries, which she did," D.J. said. "And now he wants to get rid of her because she did what he told her to do? That doesn't make sense."

"You think Spencer knows something about the deaths of Maxine Porter, Karen Nelson, and Carla Garcia," Sione said. "Well, maybe Ben thinks so, too. Maybe Ben doesn't want Spencer to tell the cops what she knows about the murders because she knows those women are dead because of Ben."

It wasn't an outright lie, Sione told himself. Maxine Porter, Karen Nelson, and Carla Garcia had been killed because of the deal they'd made with Ben. Technically, Ben bore some responsibility because he'd convinced the women to go against Richard. A stupid mistake that had cost them their lives.

What he'd told his cousin wasn't too damn far from the truth, but he couldn't tell D.J. anything about Moana.

How could he explain that Moana hadn't died in some prison fight? How could he explain that Moana's demise had been orchestrated by Richard, who'd helped her fake her death so she could get out of jail and kill for him? A claim Sione still found hard to accept and damn near impossible to believe.

"I think Ben wants to get rid of Spencer so she won't go to the police."

"All right, fine," D.J. said. "Give me the address to the house in Shawville. I'll go back there and take a look around. Maybe I can find something that might give us an idea of where she is."

36

Night descended. Thick blackness poured into the small, hot room, filling every corner and crevice. Not even a sliver of light from the moon managed to make its way through the window. The darkness converged on Spencer, as though it had swallowed her whole. Painful memories contaminated her mind.

Spencer felt like she was seven years old again, alone in the dark apartment, scared, sad, and confused. After her mother had left her, the sound of the door slamming ricocheted in her head, terrifying and confusing. She didn't understand why her mother had left. She had been afraid something bad had happened to her mother.

Bugs chirped and buzzed, whizzing by her face. She whipped her head left and right, unable to swat them away. Insects landed on her skin, and she was forced to jerk and twitch to get the unseen bugs off her. The smell of damp earth and stale urine assaulted her nostrils.

Night sounds abounded, a swelling chorus of rustling, scurrying, and scampering.

She closed her eyes and drew her knees up to her chest, praying through her tears that she would be rescued, even if maybe she didn't deserve to be saved—even if this was her punishment for all her mistakes. She prayed she wouldn't die, alone and abandoned, in the small, hot room.

Terrorized, she imagined her dead body would be left behind by Tommy Fong and soon forgotten, left for the vultures that would pick at her skin and muscle until she was nothing but bones. A skeleton bleached by the sun, she would be found years after her death, accidentally stumbled upon by tourists. Her remains would go unidentified, while miles away, her sisters would always wonder what had happened to her. Rae and Shady would hold out hope for her return and yet know in their hearts that they would never see her again.

Leaning her head against the wall behind her, Spencer sobbed bitterly, vehemently.

She would have faded from John's memory. He would have moved on. He would have found a woman to be Mrs. Tuiali'i and had children with her. Spencer would never cross his mind. He would have given up trying to figure out what had happened to her.

Had he already given up, Spencer wondered.

By now, John had to know she was missing. She hadn't come home from the art show. Did he suspect something bad had happened? Or did he think she was some criminal who'd had to flee Belize because she'd learned the cops were on her trail?

Shivering, despite the humidity, Spencer thought back to the day when she'd first met John. He'd beat up Tommy Fong for her, and he hadn't even known her. He had fought for her. No other man had ever done that before.

John had been willing to fight her battles, even though he hadn't known if she was worth the trouble or not. He was the kind of guy girls dreamed of meeting but never did. Not just tall and good-looking, but brave and compassionate, a man who did keep his promises, it turned out.

John was the kind of guy she might actually become "that wife" for.

37

"Where your boyfriend, bitch?" Tommy Fong teased, goading her. "Why he not come to save you yet?"

Dawn had broken as night slowly faded away, leaving behind a pall of gloom. Spencer realized she must have slept despite the insects, the darkness, and the cacophony of buzzing and scurrying.

Opening her eyes, Spencer stared at Fong. He stood near the door, holding a large plastic bowl in one hand and a bottle of water in the other. He walked to the mattress, crouched down, and then sat in the dirt, legs folded. Shrinking away from him, Spencer eyed the contents of the bowl.

Fruit. Chunks of pineapple mixed with slices of banana. Her stomach responded, growling. When was the last time she'd eaten? She didn't really remember. She didn't even know how long she'd been in the small, hot room. Two days? Three? Forever?

Fong twisted the cap off the bottle of water and held the opening toward her. "Drink."

Spencer turned her face away, though she was thirsty and her mouth dry. She didn't trust him and was surprised by, and suspicious of, his gesture. How could a man who'd beat her to within an inch of her life offer her water to quench her thirst? And how could she accept after his brutal cruelty?

Still, she parted her lips and allowed the lukewarm water to stream into her mouth. After she drank half the bottle, Fong took it away, replaced the cap, and set the bottle next to the mattress. He picked up the bowl of fruit.

"I'm not hungry," she said, having already decided she would refuse the food despite her stomach's rumblings. It could be spoiled or contaminated, teeming with some microscopic bug. Last thing she needed was a case of the runs.

"You got to eat, bitch," he said, spearing a piece of pineapple with a plastic fork he pulled from the pocket of his dirty, weather-beaten jeans. "You cannot starve to death. You no good dead."

"What are you talking about?" She stared at him, cautioning herself against any rising hopes. His words seemed to suggest he needed to keep her alive for some reason. But she had doubts. He could be lying. He might still kill her. "What do you mean I'm no good if I'm dead?"

"Eat," he insisted, thrusting the pineapple toward her mouth.

Wary, Spencer opened her mouth and clamped her teeth down on the chunk of fruit, pulled it from the plastic tines, and chewed. After she swallowed, she asked, "Why did you kidnap me?"

"No questions." He stabbed a slice of banana and then held it inches from her mouth. "Eat."

She accepted the banana, chewed, swallowed, and then asked, "Did Ben tell you to kidnap me?"

"Not Ben," Fong grunted.

"It wasn't Ben?" Spencer stared at him, her pulse jumping. "Then who the hell was it? Who told you to—"

"Richard," Fong said. "He the Goddamn devil."

Spencer stared at him, a strange jolt slicing through her.

Richard. She knew the "Goddamn devil" Fong was talking about. Maxine Porter and the blonde tomboy had told her about him. As far as Spencer knew, Richard had no idea who she was.

"Why did Richard tell you to kidnap me?"

"Richard give Ben an order," Fong continued. "Ben do not want to follow the order, so Richard got to make him mind. Ben have to learn to be obedient. Richard teach him."

"How?"

"No more questions."

"Tell me," Spencer said, moving her head when he tried to feed her another pineapple chunk. "How is Richard going to teach Ben to be obedient?"

"Richard take away something very important to Ben," Fong said. "Something Ben care about very much."

"That's why you broke into Ben's house that night," Spencer said, remembering what Ben had told her.

Tommy Fong just glared at her.

Persistent, her heart slamming, Spencer asked, "What were you trying to take from Ben that night?"

"You."

38

Sione woke to a voice he wished wasn't so familiar, a voice he could never forget.

Yesterday, after D.J. left, he'd holed up in a bedroom at the back of the house and waited. Time passed and night fell. Sione dozed but couldn't really rest. He was too agitated, too angry and apprehensive to sleep.

He couldn't really sleep without Spencer, anyway. He wasn't sure how he'd gotten to the point where he couldn't close his eyes unless she was in his arms, but he was there. And he didn't want to leave, didn't want things to change.

Rubbing his face, Sione blinked, then rose slowly from the chair, and walked to the bedroom door. Opening it a crack, he listened. Voices raised in anger and confusion. One of the voices was unfamiliar but was probably Bermudez. The other voice belonged to a man he would always despise.

Ben Chang.

The men were shouting at each other and over each other, neither allowing the other a word in edgewise. The voices grew louder, desperate words in a language he'd heard before but wasn't able to make sense of.

Sione cursed under his breath. Bermudez and Ben were speaking Jamaican patois. He understood Jamaican patois just as well as he understood island pidgin which was not at all. Couldn't make out a damn word. Couldn't even pick up the context of their conversation. For all he knew, they could have been discussing the price of tea in China.

Hearing Ben's voice conjured up a host of emotions. Hatred ... because of what happened between Ben and Moana. Jealousy ... Ben's relationship with Richard bothered him in ways he didn't want to admit. There was an envy Sione was reluctant to acknowledge. Richard was the father Ben had always wanted, but for Sione, Richard was the father who'd failed him.

Sione wondered what life might have been like if he and Ben had stayed close. He and Ben would never be friends again, but they would always be connected. Richard was the tie that bound them together, and the tie was wound so tight, it was almost impossible to sever.

Cursing himself, Sione took a deep breath. What the hell was his problem? Why the hell was he still standing there when he should have been confronting Ben about having Spencer kidnapped, choking the truth from the son of a bitch?

Yanking the bedroom door open wider, Sione crossed the threshold and headed into the hall. He could tell Ben was pissed about something. Bermudez sounded contrite and conciliatory. Anxious to wrap his hands around Ben's throat, Sione walked around the corner and into the living room.

Abruptly, Sione stopped, confused.

Alone in the living room, Bermudez sat on the couch staring at something on the coffee table in front of him.

Ben was still yelling, still spewing rapid-fire Patois, and yet he wasn't in the living room. Not physically, Sione realized, his gaze drawn to the small object on the coffee table.

A cell phone.

Bermudez was talking to Ben on a cell phone, and obviously had him on 'Speaker'. His voice barely above a whisper, Bermudez responded to Ben's terse demands. Unfocused, not sure what to do, Sione listened as Ben wrapped up his tirade. Bermudez stabbed a finger against the screen, ending the call.

Consumed with rage and disappointment, Sione stalked over to Bermudez and grabbed the cell phone. "Call Ben back," he demanded. "Get him on the phone now!"

Cowering, startled and confused, Bermudez said, "I can't. I don't know his number, he don't—"

Sione slammed the cell phone against Bermudez's ear. The man screamed, and tried to scramble off the couch, but Sione grabbed him around the throat, squeezing his trachea. Twitching and gasping, Bermudez struggled, digging his heels into the large area rug, trying to claw at Sione's hand. Sione tightened his hold around Bermudez's throat, pinning him back against the couch cushion.

"Stop struggling," Sione said. "You're only making it worse."

Bermudez continued to wiggle, trying in vain to move Sione's hand.

"I'm going to move my hand a bit so you can breathe." Sione yanked Bermudez forward. "And then you are going to answer my questions, but if you try anything, I will break your neck. Do you understand me?"

Bermudez nodded, and Sione removed his hand. Coughing, Bermudez rubbed his throat, glaring at Sione.

Sione crossed his arms and stared at the sweat-soaked son of a bitch. "What the hell happened to Spencer?"

Bermudez coughed again and then said, "Tommy Fong took her."

"Who the hell is Tommy Fong?" Sione asked, frustrated.

"Triad enforcer," Bermudez said. "Bastard got a green snake tattoo on his face. Been beefing with Ben for a long time."

"So Fong took Spencer because of some beef he has with Ben?" Sione asked.

Dark eyes cold, Bermudez stared at him. "No, he took her because Richard told him to."

"*Richard* told Fong to take Spencer?" Sione glared at Bermudez. "You're lying. That's not true."

"It is true," Bermudez said. "Richard told Fong to kidnap Ms. Edwards."

"Why?" Sione asked, struggling to focus, feeling like he'd been kicked in the head.

"Your father wanted to teach Mr. Chang a lesson."

"What kind of lesson?"

"Richard don't like to be disobeyed," Bermudez said. "There is consequences for disobedience. That's why Richard told Fong to take Ms. Edwards."

"How the hell is kidnapping Spencer a consequence for Ben's disobedience?"

"You know what happens when you disobey Richard," Bermudez said. "He hurts the people you care about. That way, you learn not to go against him. You learn to do what he tell you to do."

"Why the hell would Ben care about Spencer?" Sione demanded.

Bermudez glanced up at him. "What makes you think Mr. Chang don't care about her?"

"He doesn't even know her," Sione said.

"You sure about that?"

Sione stared at Bermudez, confused and apprehensive. Spencer had told him she didn't know Ben was the payday loan business owner who forced her to come to Belize and deliver money and fake passports. Maybe that wasn't true. Maybe Spencer did know Ben and what he was involved in. Maybe she was an active and willing participant.

The question was, did he really want to know for sure? And if Spencer had lied to him, would he care? Should he care? Bermudez had invoked suspicions Sione didn't want to deal with, suspicions he didn't want confirmed. He could live with suspicions, though.

But could he live with truth?

The truth could get in the way of what he wanted, hinder his chance to have something real and lasting with Spencer. But if the truth was that she'd lied to him about knowing Ben Chang, then …

Then … *what?*

How could he be angry with Spencer for lying to him when he was lying to her? He hadn't been honest about his own connection to Ben Chang. How could he be hypocritical and demand full disclosure from her?

Sione glared at Bermudez. "What were you and Ben talking about?"

A wet, sputtering cough escaped Bermudez's lips, and then he said, "He wanted to know where Ms. Edwards was. I told him Fong took her. He asked me where Fong was, and I told him."

"You told Ben where to find Spencer?" Sione asked. "Why the hell would you do that? If Ben hurts her, I'm going to kill him, and then I'm going to kill you."

Flinching, Bermudez shook his head. "He ain't gonna hurt her."

"How the hell do you know that?"

"Because Ms. Edwards got something that Mr. Chang wants."

"What are you talking about?"

"Don't know what it is," Bermudez said. "But he sent her here to get it for him."

"Ben sent her to Belize to deliver money and fake passports to three women," Sione said. "And all three of those women ended up dead."

"Mr. Chang ain't killed them."

A strange jolt passed through Sione. Bermudez wasn't lying. Ben Chang hadn't killed Carla Garcia, Maxine Porter, and Karen Nelson. Moana had fired the fatal bullets. Then Sione had killed Moana —maybe.

"Mr. Chang ain't gonna kill Ms. Edwards," Bermudez insisted. "She got something he needs."

"Well, since you know where Tommy Fong is staying," Sione said and then grabbed Bermudez by the throat and yanked him off the couch, "you're going to take me to him."

Cursing, Bermudez tried to pry Sione's hand away, gagging and tripping over his feet as Sione forced him toward the door. Sione grabbed the knob with his left hand and opened the door. Sliding his hand to the back of Bermudez's neck, he forced the man over the threshold, onto the concrete porch, and then down the three steps. Beyond the corrugated awning covering the porch, the sun was bright, harsh, and hot.

Sione guided Bermudez toward the fence, and they walked along the waist-high chain-link separating the yard from the tangle of trees and bushes on the opposite side.

They were yards from the paved road in front of the property when an SUV turned into the gravel-and-grass driveway. The vehicle stopped a few feet away. Squinting, Sione shielded his eyes from the glare of sunlight off the windshield of the SUV.

Seconds later, the driver's door of the SUV opened. D.J. got out and then stalked toward him, scowling, churning up gravel and dust with each long, determined stride.

"What the hell?" D.J. demanded. "What are you doing?"

"A guy named Tommy Fong took Spencer," Sione said, keeping his hold on Bermudez. "This asshole knows where Fong is staying, and—"

"Why didn't you call me?" D.J. asked. "When I left you last night, we agreed that—"

Sione said, "I know what we agreed to, but—"

"If I hadn't decided to call Jared and come over here to see what the hell was going on," D.J. said, "then you would have gone off without me, on your own, with no backup, or—"

"I don't have time to argue with you," Sione said. "I need to get to Spencer."

The passenger door slammed. Sione glanced toward the SUV. Jared walked around the front of the SUV, toward Sione and D.J. "Somebody want to tell me what the hell is going on?"

"I know where Spencer is, and I need to get to her," Sione told Jared. "Ben is already on his way there."

"Ben?" Jared stared at Sione. "Ben Chang? What the hell does he have to do with all this?"

Sione shook his head. "I don't have time to explain."

Jared said, "You better make time."

"After I get Spencer back," Sione said.

"You can't go up against Ben by yourself," D.J. said.

"I'm not afraid of Ben Chang," Sione said.

"I know you're not," D.J. said. "But you're not thinking straight.

And I don't want you to let these misguided feelings for Ms. Edwards make you do something stupid, like kill Ben Chang."

"If you insist on running off to rescue Ms. Edwards," Jared said, "then we're coming with you."

39

"Sweet girl ..." The whispered voice terrified Spencer, the sound sinking into her, leaving her confused and unable to move. "Wake up ..."

Spencer ignored the light taps against her cheek. She prayed the nightmare would be over soon and her dreams of John would return. John was the only man she wanted. The man she'd always wanted. She just hadn't known it.

Spencer hadn't allowed herself to believe she deserved someone like John. A man willing to love her despite her flaws and faults. A man who accepted and understood that she made mistakes but wouldn't hold them against her or punish her because she wasn't perfect. Keeping her eyes shut, Spencer prayed that when she opened them John would be there, gazing at her with those beautiful hazel eyes.

She needed John to be there. She wanted to tell him how she felt about him. She needed so badly to tell him—

"Sweet girl!" The voice was forceful, commanding. "You have to get up!"

Angry, her hopes dashed, Spencer opened her eyes. A sob escaped, but she bit her lip and rubbed her eyes, refusing to cry. Ben sat beside her on the edge of the mattress.

"What are you doing here?"

"Doing for you what you refused to do for me, sweet girl." He pulled her to a sitting position. "I'm saving your life. I'm not leaving you to die."

"How did you find me?" Spencer asked. "How did you know I was here?"

"That doesn't matter," he said and then grabbed her hands and held them up.

"What are you doing?"

Instead of answering her, Ben held up a knife and sliced the rope Fong had tied her with. Seconds later, he slit the rope that held her ankles, and she was free of the restraints.

"Come on." Ben grabbed her hand and pulled her to her feet.

"Why did you trick me?" Spencer yanked her hand from his firm grasp, terror and rage dueling within her, fighting to dominate her emotions. "Why did you make me think you were going to be at that house?"

Ben sighed. "I don't know what you're talking about, but—"

"You know exactly what I'm talking about!" she said. "You sent me a note telling me to meet you, but when I got to the house, you weren't there! It was that crazy asshole Tommy Fong!"

"I don't know anything about some note Fong sent you," Ben said, dismissive. "Tell me where the envelope is."

Backing away from him, she said, "The envelope?"

"Sweet girl." Frowning, Ben took a step toward her. "I need that envelope. You sent me several texts saying that you had found the envelope and you wanted to meet so we could make an exchange."

"Tommy Fong almost killed me and all you care about is that damn envelope?"

Ben frowned at her. "The envelope is not all I care about. But you were supposed to find that envelope, which you did, so now I—"

"Where have you been?" Spencer stared up at him, confused and furious. "Why didn't you return any of my texts? I didn't know what had happened to you. I didn't know if you were alive or dead!"

"Is that a bit of concern in your tone, sweet girl?" Ben asked, an amused smirk playing at the corner of his mouth. "Were you worried about me?"

Spencer looked away, not sure what to think or say, still groggy and disoriented. Closing her eyes, she took a deep breath, wishing it wasn't so damn hot and muggy. Her hair hung around her shoulders, the strands limp and damp. Sweat rolled from her neck, down her back, and between her breasts.

"No, I didn't think so," Ben said. "If you were worried about anything, it was getting your hands on that video."

"I don't know where the envelope is," Spencer said, looking away, not in the mood to feel condemned for wanting to avoid prison or guilty about the things she'd done to stay out of jail.

"What do you mean you don't know?" Ben glared at her. "Your messages said that you found the envelope and—"

"I did find it," she said, rubbing her eyes, trying to get her bearings. "When I got that fake message from Tommy Fong, I put the envelope in my purse. But I don't know where my purse is. "

"Why don't you know—"

"When I got to the house Fong told me to come to," Spencer said, "he attacked me, and all I could think was I had to get out of there. I think I accidentally dropped my purse. I wasn't thinking about anything except getting away from Fong before he killed me."

Rubbing his chin, Ben said, "He wouldn't have killed you."

"He said that, too," Spencer said. "He told me I was no good dead. What did he mean by that?"

"Sweet girl, listen to me. We need to leave," Ben said. "We need to go back to the house Fong told you to go to last night. Can you remember where the house is?"

"I'm not going back to that house," she said, sidestepping away from him, glancing around the small, humid shed, looking for a weapon.

"That's where you left your purse, remember?" Ben said, his calm tone laced with barely suppressed irritation. "And you put the envelope in your purse, so we have to go back to that house and—"

"That's where Tommy Fong attacked me! Because of you!" Spencer screamed at him. "Because Richard wanted to make you behave! I was taken so you could learn to be obedient! That's why I went through this hell!"

"Sweet girl, what are you talking about?" Ben glared at her.

"I thought I was going to die!" she screamed at him. "I was treated worse than a dog because you disobeyed an order!"

"No man gives me orders!" Ben thundered.

"Richard gives you orders!" She took another step back. "If you had obeyed them, this wouldn't have happened to me!"

"You don't know what you're talking about," he said. "We need to go!"

"I'm not going anywhere with you!" she said.

"Sweet girl, you have to trust me!"

"Trust you!" she screamed. "You threatened to kill my grandmother! As soon as you get what you want, you'll kill me, too! Just like you killed Maxine Porter and Carla Garcia and—"

"Listen to me!" Ben grabbed her and shook her so hard, her teeth rattled. "If I wanted you dead, I would have killed you a long time ago! I could have done it the last time we made love. Don't you remember that night? And the next morning?"

"I woke up to a knife in my face!"

"Did I cut you?" Ben asked. "Did I slit your throat? I could have put that knife in your chest while you were sleeping next to me! But I didn't, and do you know why? Because I love you, Spencer!"

Shocked, she stared at him. *Spencer?* Her stomach jerked, and she felt something within her began to plummet. Since when had Ben ever called her Spencer? From the first day she'd met him, she'd been his *sweet girl*, not Spencer.

When he said her name, it was as though he was talking to someone else, talking about someone else. It didn't sound natural coming from his mouth. It made him seem like a stranger.

I love you, Spencer.

That wasn't true. She didn't believe it. She wouldn't believe it.

"Why do you look so surprised?" he asked. "Don't you know by now how I feel about you?"

Confused, Spencer shook her head. "I don't understand. How can you say—"

The door burst open, banging against the wall. Ben released her and turned, blocking her view. Spencer took a few side steps to the left. Tommy Fong stood in the doorway.

Glaring at Ben, Fong growled a series of harsh words Spencer didn't understand but knew were Chinese. Ben replied in Chinese. Fong spoke again, his voice wavering with furious accusation. Stabbing a finger at Fong, Ben let forth a litany of phrases. She knew they were curses, and while not directed at her, they affected her as though they were, chilling her to the core.

Ben's epithets seemed to have manifested into something sinister.

The unseen terror appeared to grab Tommy Fong around the throat. Eyes wide, petrified, the small, wiry Asian turned and fled.

Ben faced her. "Stay here," he said and then took off, following Tommy Fong and slamming the door behind him.

Confused, she stared at the door, feeling forlorn and abandoned.

Seconds later, there was a crash, something banging and tumbling, hitting the floor. Spencer went rigid, listening, trying to make out the sounds beyond the closed door. What the hell was happening? Were Ben and Tommy Fong fighting? Were they killing each other?

A wild, hoarse cry startled her, sending her heart into her throat.

A gunshot echoed.

Her heart racing, Spencer ran to the door, and without thinking, she flung it open.

In the living room near the coffee table, Fong crawled slowly across the floor, coughing and spitting blood, heading toward the front door. Ben stood over him, the muscles in his arm contracting as he lowered the gun in his hand until the barrel was aimed at Fong's legs.

Gasping softly, Spencer held her breath. Ben muttered more words in Chinese. The gun went off again, abrupt and deafening, shaking her from the inside out. Fong screamed. Seconds later, another gunshot blasted. The report reverberated off the walls, mixing with the hoarse, strangled cries of Fong as bullets slammed into his legs.

Horrified, Spencer slammed the door and leaned against it, trying to get her bearings, trying to breathe, trying to think. She couldn't just stand there and do nothing. She had to move. She had to get the hell out of the house. Her gaze flitted around the room, scanning objects, sizing them up, judging each as a potential tool for escape. Her eyes locked on a shovel leaning against a wall. If she hurled it at the window with all the strength she had left, it might break the glass panes.

A door slammed. Startled, Spencer turned, ran back to the door she'd closed, and opened it. In the living room, Tommy Fong was on the floor, moaning and writhing. Ben was gone. Spencer glanced around the living room, confused. Where had Ben gone? What was happening?

"Help me …" Fong whispered. "Help me … gun … need the gun."

Spencer glared at him. Help him? Was he insane? He'd beat her and tied her up like an animal and he expected her to help him?

"The gun …" Fong rasped. "Table …"

Spencer spotted the gun on the coffee table and dashed to it. Grabbing the gun, Spencer ran back into the small, hot room. A door slammed again.

Seconds later, she heard, "You like to tie women up, huh?"

Ben was back. Gripping the gun, Spencer crept toward the door and stared out into the living room. Holding a red plastic gas can, Ben was walking around Tommy Fong, pouring gasoline on him as Fong writhed and cried, struggling to crawl away from the liquid splashing down around him, soaking his clothes and hair. Gagging from the smell of gasoline wafting in the air, Spencer watched, horrified, and yet mesmerized, as Ben doused Fong's body with the gas.

"Did Richard tell you to tie her up?" Ben asked, staring down at Fong. "Did he tell you to beat her?"

Terrified, Spencer waited, her heart slamming as Ben reached into the pocket of his trousers and pulled out a matchbook. Growling words in Chinese, Ben struck the match and dropped it onto Fong. Screams filled the air as flames leaped across Fong's body. Spencer turned from the hellish scene. Panicked and frantic, she didn't know what to do, didn't know what to think.

"Sweet girl …"

Spencer spun around. Ben stood in the doorway, staring at her.

"Stay back!" She raised the gun, pointing it at him, shocked at the weight of it. "Get away from the door and stay back!"

"Give me the gun before you hurt yourself," he said, walking toward her.

"Get away from me!" Spencer ordered, the gun wobbling in her trembling hands. "I mean it, get away from me or I will put a bullet between your eyes!"

"Sweet girl." Ben sighed and shook his head. "There's no way your aim could be that good. I doubt you even know how to shoot a gun."

"How hard can it be?" she asked, infuriated, terrified, and knowing he was right. She would aim at him and somehow end up shooting herself. "All I have to do is pull the trigger."

"Instead of trying to shoot me," Ben said. "Why don't we go and get your purse so you can give me the envelope and I can give you the video?"

"I don't need the video!" Spencer said, tightening her death grip on the pistol. "I'm going to tell the police what you did, and you're going to prison for murder!"

"What are you talking about?"

"You just killed Tommy Fong! You burned him alive!"

His gaze curious, Ben took a step toward her. "Have you thought about what will happen if the cops come and arrest me?"

"Stay back," Spencer warned, stepping backward.

"Eventually, I'll go to trial, and you'll have to testify against me."

Keeping her eyes on him, Spencer tried to anticipate the sudden move she feared he would soon make.

"The police will want to know why I killed Tommy Fong," Ben

said. "And you will have to tell them that I blackmailed you because you stole from me."

"Shut up!" She gripped the gun, struggling to keep it aimed at his face, feeling as though a noose had been slipped over her head, and Ben was steadily tightening the rope, making it impossible for her to breathe.

He was right, and she hated him for it.

"I will corroborate your story," Ben said. "I will show the police the tape of you stealing from me. And what will Sione think about that? Doesn't that worry you?"

Spencer wished she wasn't worried. She wished she wasn't terrified of what would happen if John ever found out about her "dating," those awful things she'd never really wanted to do and had only done out of desperation. She wanted to be able to count on John's feelings for her. But she didn't know for sure that what she and John had was secure and stable, unable to be torn apart by the truth about her lies.

"When Sione finds out the treacherous bitch you really are—"

"Shut up!"

"You think you can explain to Sione why you stole from me? You think you can make him understand?" Ben asked, glaring at her. "You really think he wants to find out that this beautiful woman he is falling in love with is a heartless criminal who drugs men and steals from them? Think of how disappointed and disillusioned he would be. How could he ever trust you? Every time you fixed him a drink, he would think twice before he—"

"Go to hell!"

"Come on, sweet girl," Ben chided. "Think rationally. You have Sione. He wants to be with you, he may already be in love with you, and if not, then he is very close to being in love with you."

"I doubt that," Spencer said, wondering if she could dare to believe John had fallen for her.

"You're so close to getting what you want. Don't blow it now, sweet girl," Ben told her. "You need to think of yourself, think of the life Sione can give you. You can't let this opportunity slip away. You may never get this chance again."

Wary, she stared at him. He was right. She couldn't let the opportunity to be with John slip through her fingers. And yet, she still had to think it all through. She had to make the right decision.

"Sweet girl, listen to me." Ben edged closer. "You need to let me go. Then you can live happily ever after with Sione. Isn't that what you want?"

She did want that, but she didn't know how she felt about Ben giving her the chance to make a life with John. She wasn't sure what that once-in-a-lifetime chance would cost her, but she suspected the payment might be her sanity, her dignity, and her independence.

But what had her fierce self-reliance profited her? Nothing she could boast about. Why hold on to it? Spencer wanted to be with John. She wanted him to protect her and take care of her. She wanted him to do all the things she'd never wanted, or trusted, a man to do for her.

"There is no time to waste, sweet girl," he said, walking toward her. "What are you going to do?"

"Stay back," she warned, panicked. "Don't come any closer, or I will—"

"You'll what?" Ben stopped a few feet away from her. "You'll shoot me? And leave me for dead, again? That's what a treacherous bitch like you does, right? But you remember this, sweet girl … the robbery of the wicked shall destroy them."

"Get away from me." She took a step back, keeping the gun aimed at his face.

Smiling, Ben started toward her again, saying, "... and whoso diggeth a pit shall fall therein ..."

"I mean it, Ben, stay away." She took another backward step, slipping, gasping as she struggled to stay on her feet.

"The way of the wicked is as darkness, they know not at what they stumble ..."

Two more quick steps backward and she felt herself pressed against something hard and unmovable. Ben had backed her into the wall. He was still coming toward her, and she knew he wouldn't stop.

"The wicked worketh a deceitful work—"

Terrified, Spencer squeezed the trigger.

40

There was a hollow click.

Shaking and bewildered, Spencer pulled the trigger again. Another hollow click, and her heart sank. The gunshot she'd expected to deafen her ears didn't come, but another sound caught her attention for a moment. Faint and distant, it seemed to be like—

"I knew you couldn't shoot me, sweet girl." Ben yanked the gun away from her, threw it onto the mattress, and then grabbed her. "Not without bullets."

"Get away from me!" Spencer tried to push him away as he clamped an arm around her back, pinning her against him. "Sonofabitch, you knew that gun was empty!"

Ben stared at her, giving her his sly smile.

"And you just stood there and let me point an empty gun at you," she said, trying to yank away from his iron grip.

"Even if the gun had been loaded," Ben said, "you still wouldn't have shot me. You would have let me go because you want this fantasy with Sione so desperately."

As she tried to twist away, the faint sound grew louder, and Spencer realized what she was hearing—tires on gravel. Tires ... a car? Was someone—

"Sione is not what you think, sweet girl," Ben told her. "You think he's your knight in shining armor, but the truth is, we are more alike than we are different."

"You're nothing like John," she said. "He is good and decent, and he wouldn't force me to pay for my mistakes over and over—"

"Sione would never forgive you if you made a mistake, sweet girl," Ben pulled her close, caressing her cheek. "He would never understand your choices, and he would condemn you for them, but I understand why you made those mistakes, and I do forgive you."

She tilted her head back, giving him an invitation, but to what, she wasn't sure. And yet, he took her offer...

As soon as he put his lips on hers, something strange claimed her, and for a moment, she felt like the sad girl sitting on the bench in front of the reflecting pool, and all she wanted was for him to be the man she'd thought he was, the man who would protect her and take care of her.

She felt his hands moving up and down her back, and when he slipped his tongue into her mouth, she wasn't sure if she wanted to push him away. She heard a soft slam. Then another slam seconds later and then a third slam.

Breaking the kiss, Ben stepped back a bit, withdrawing his embrace. "Well, sweet girl, sounds like we might have some visitors."

The words were barely out of Ben's mouth when there was a wild, desperate banging on the front door.

"Spencer!" It was a muffled, demanding cry. "Spencer! Are you in there!"

"Well, well, well," Ben said. "Your hero is here, sweet girl."

Panic and relief surging through her, Spencer froze, afraid to believe what she'd heard, afraid she was just wishing and hoping and praying John had come. Looking toward the opened door leading into the living room, Spencer turned from Ben, anxious to let John know she was there and alive and grateful to God that he had come to rescue her.

"Not so fast, sweet girl." Ben grabbed her and pulled her back to him.

Trembling, she gazed up at him, waiting, wondering what his final words to her would be, unsure what she wanted to hear.

"You still owe me," Ben said. "And you will pay for your mistakes. I won't let you get away with what you did to me. But, fortunately for you, right now is not the best time for vengeance."

Spencer stared at him, hoping there was some defiance in her gaze and not the fear she felt, the trepidation caused by the amused malice in his dark eyes.

"So, here is what's going to happen. I'm going to get out of here. After Sione breaks that door down and comes rushing in here to save you, he'll probably ask you what happened, and I don't really care what you tell him. I'm sure a treacherous, deceptive bitch like you will think of a good lie. But keep my name out of it. Don't tell anyone that I was here or what I did to Fong. Don't make problems for me, and I won't make problems for you, sweet girl."

41

"Spencer ..."

She felt a hand close over hers, fingers slipping between her fingers. At once, everything within her started to lift. Trembling and dizzy with relief and happiness, Spencer tilted her head back to look up at him.

"John ..." she whispered back, afraid it might not really be him, but then he put his arm around her, helping her up from the mattress where she'd collapsed after Ben had fled the small, humid room, escaping through the window.

Exhausted and horrified, she'd been left to deal with Ben's threats and taunts, lingering in the stale, hot air like evil spirits.

You still owe me ... you will pay for your mistakes ... you won't get away with what you did to me.

When John pulled her close to him, all the terror and tribulation vanished. Crying, Spencer pressed her face against his chest and then wrapped her arms around him.

"It's okay." John rubbed a hand up and down her back, kissing the top of her head, soothing her. "You're going to be okay ... you're safe, okay ... I'm here now ..."

42

San Ignacio, Belize

Belizean Banyan Resort - Owner's Casita

Humming to herself, Spencer removed a carafe of fresh pineapple juice from the sub-zero refrigerator and took it to the island in the center of the kitchen. Still humming, she pirouetted across the sun-dappled kitchen to the row of overhead cabinets near the sink and got two glasses.

It was a gorgeous morning. Abundant sunlight flooded the kitchen, a warm, golden glow, brightening every corner, gleaming across every surface, and bringing a smile to her face.

Sometimes, she couldn't believe how lucky she was. Blessed was what her sister Shady would tell her. And she did feel her current happiness was due to divine intervention. Whatever it was, she was thankful and delightfully surprised.

If anyone had told her she would be standing in this kitchen, happy and content, she would have thought they were out of their mind. Here she was, six months later, happy and content.

The one thing she'd never wanted was the reason for her current state of mind. Love. Falling in love, specifically. She'd been afraid of it and had vowed not to do it. And yet love had claimed her and she was glad. Now she and John were together, and she was starting to believe forever was possible for them. She was starting to believe happily ever after wasn't just a silly fairytale; fantasy was a reality for her.

Six months had given them time to get to know each other, exploring and examining each other from as many different angles as possible and gaining new perspectives based on what they'd learned.

Being open and vulnerable, sharing elements of her life she usually tried to forget, had been daunting. John had been more willing to expose himself, but at times the ability proved difficult and frustrating for him, as well.

They'd persevered and discussed a myriad of topics from their early childhood to their favorite colors. In between, they spoke about their hopes, dreams, likes, and dislikes. The result was a greater appreciation of each other's emotions, motives, preferences, and overall outlook on life. There was also a more profound understanding of how they each dealt with issues, problems, and obstacles. And they'd figured out what annoyed and irritated them about each other.

John didn't like her independent streak or her sparks of self-reliance. She couldn't stand his "hero" tendencies and his need to rescue people from problems of their own making.

Being together all this time hadn't been just love and scorching hot sex and spooning on the couch. They were both strong-willed and opinionated, and their disagreements could be as fiery and ferocious as their lovemaking.

Despite the occasional heated discussion, Spencer loved him more than she ever thought she could, maybe even more than she should. She was determined to make the relationship last forever no matter what she had to do.

The only threat to their happiness was maybe their own secrets. There were things John hadn't told her about himself, though he'd hinted at a past life he wasn't proud of. She could never tell John about the "dating." He wouldn't understand and he wouldn't forgive her. They had an unspoken agreement not to discuss these secrets because they'd decided the past didn't matter.

But Ben still had the power to destroy her life. Ben knew things about her that she never wanted John to find out. John wouldn't find out as long as Spencer kept her mouth shut about what had happened in the small, humid room.

Don't make problems for me, and I won't make problems for you, sweet girl.

After the horror of the small, humid room, Spencer had been thoroughly interrogated by John's cousins, D.J. and Jared, the San Ignacio detective, who had joined John on his quest to rescue her.

Spencer wasn't sure if they believed her story, but she'd stuck to it. She had been kidnapped by Tommy Fong, though she wasn't sure why. And she had no idea who had killed Fong because she'd been locked in the small, humid room when he was being burned alive.

Spencer poured pineapple juice into a glass. It felt like forever since she'd seen Ben, since he'd walked out of the tiny, hot room and out of her life. She still thought about him—probably more than she should have.

She never knew what might spark a memory of him. Sometimes it would be a stray breeze slanting across her nose, carrying the smell of allspice, the formation of a puffy white cloud, or the dark sensual beauty of a black orchid. Suddenly, she would remember the tall, handsome man with the sly, hypnotic smile. She would wonder how those fantasies she had of him had turned into nightmares. Ben wasn't gone for good, though, she was sure of that.

You still owe me …

Her debt was still outstanding. But, she could make the payment. She had the damn envelope Ben had forced her to find. It was still in the blue Birkin, hidden at the bottom where she'd put it that night, so many months ago, when she'd left the resort to deliver the envelope to Ben.

A week after the kidnapping ordeal, John had told her about finding the purse and how it was, to him, the most compelling proof that something bad had happened to her.

She stared at the pineapple juice, a sudden sense of unease settling over her. Sometimes, she had the feeling that her suffering wouldn't end once she gave Ben the envelope and he gave her the damning video. She worried that following their unholy exchange, whenever it happened, something worse would happen to her, something far more terrifying.

And Ben would be the architect of that terror.

You will pay for your mistakes … you won't get away with what you did to me.

It wasn't just a threat. It was a promise.

Arms circled her waist from the back, interrupting thoughts she had no business indulging in anyway, and seconds later, Spencer felt lips on her neck, brushing across her skin. Giggling, she looked up over her shoulder.

John smiled at her, his handsome face and those mesmerizing hazel eyes taking her breath away, driving all errant thoughts of Ben from her mind.

"Good morning." He lowered his head to kiss her lips, then the tip of her nose, and then both cheeks.

Smiling back at him, she turned in his embrace, facing him as he brought his mouth back to hers for a kiss that sent jolts of pleasure through her limbs, spiraling down her arms to her fingertips and swirling through her legs to her toes. John hoisted her up and onto the island; it wasn't direct eye contact, but she didn't have to break her neck looking up at him.

"So, what are your plans for the day?"

"Well, the girls have ballet," she said, wrapping her arms loosely around his neck and clasping her hands together. "And then I have to take them to the dentist. That should be fun."

John made a face.

"But, after that, I promised them I would show them how to make paper dolls."

While John went to work, most of her day was spent with his second cousins; she loved her caramel fairies as though they were her own daughters, and sometimes when they were out and about running errands, she would allow herself to pretend they were her little girls. It was a fantasy she didn't indulge in very often, and when she did, she didn't wallow in it for too long.

"Well, before you turn into Mary Poppins," John said, smiling, "I have something I want to give you."

"What?"

"Just a second," he said and then left the kitchen. He returned holding a plastic container, which contained the lush, white bloom of a flower.

"This is beautiful," she said, smiling. "What kind of flower is this?"

"Frangipani," he said, opening the container lid. "It grows on the island where I grew up, and the tradition is that a woman is supposed to wear the flower behind her right ear if she is single, and if she puts the flower behind her left ear, it means she is taken." He removed the frangipani bloom and then gave it to her, resting it in her palm.

Spencer looked at the flower and then at him.

He said, "So, I have been thinking a lot about me and you, and what's going on between us, and I know what I am hoping, but I would like you to think about us, and maybe you can let me know what you think with this flower …"

Giggling a little, she said, "Okay …"

"But don't put it on right now," he said. "Just think about me and you, and then you won't have to say anything, you can just wear the flower, and whether it's behind your left ear or your right ear, I'll know how you feel."

"How do you feel, John?" she asked. "About us?"

"Well, let's just say that …" He put one arm around her, then the other. "I'm hoping that I'll see the flower behind your left ear."

"Well, you don't have to hope," Spencer said, putting the flower behind her left ear.

Smiling, he said, "Are you sure that's how you feel?"

Nodding, Spencer wrapped her arms around his neck, kissed him, and then said, "I'm taken."

———

Spencer finally has everything she's ever wanted, but how long will her happiness last? Will she and Sione be able to withstand the final threat by Ben Chang?

Find out in the next book in the Spencer and Sione Series, Her Deadly Betrayal.

Start reading today!

ALSO BY RACHEL WOODS

REPORTER ROLAND BEAN COZY MYSTERIES

Roland "Beanie" Bean, husband and loving father, finds himself the unwitting participant in solving crimes as he seeks to make a name for himself as a reporter for the *Palmchat Gazette*.

HAPPY BIRTHDAY MURDER

EASTER EGG HUNT MURDER

MERRY CHRISTMAS MURDER

TRICK OR TREAT MURDER

GOBBLE GOBBLE MURDER

HAPPY 4TH OF JULY MURDER

PALMCHAT ISLANDS MYSTERIES

Married journalists, Vivian and Leo, manage the island newspaper while solving crimes as they chase leads for their next story.

UNTIL DEATH DO US PART

NO ONE WILL FIND YOU

YOU WILL DIE FOR THIS

DON'T MAKE ME HURT YOU

THE PALMCHAT ISLANDS MYSTERIES BOX SET: BOOKS 1 - 4

SPENCER & SIONE SERIES

Gripping romantic suspense series with steamy romance, unpredictable plot twists and devastating consequences of deceit.

HER DEADLY MISTAKE

HER DEADLY DECEPTION

HER DEADLY THREAT

HER DEADLY BETRAYAL

MURDER IN PARADISE SERIES

A series of stand-alone women sleuth mysteries with murder, mayhem and a dash of romance, set against the backdrop of turquoise waters and swaying palm trees of the fictional Palmchat Islands.

THE UNWORTHY WIFE

THE PERFECT LIAR

THE SILENT ENEMY

ABOUT THE AUTHOR

Rachel Woods studied journalism and graduated from the University of Houston where she published articles in the Daily Cougar. She is a legal assistant by day and a freelance writer and blogger with a penchant for melodrama by night. Many of her stories take place on the islands, which she has visited around the world. Rachel resides in Houston, Texas with her three sock monkeys.

For more information:
www.therachelwoods.com
rachel@therachelwoods.com

ABOUT THE PUBLISHER

BonzaiMoon Books is a family-run, artisanal publishing company created in the summer of 2014. We publish works of fiction in various genres. Our passion and focus is working with authors who write the books you want to read, and giving those authors the opportunity to have more direct input in the publishing of their work.

For more information:
www.bonzaimoonbooks.com
info@bonzaimoonbooks.com

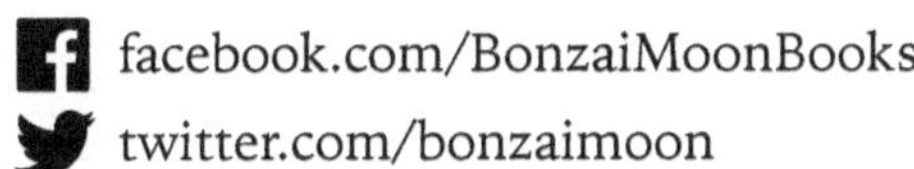